Pr...

Gun Pedersen Mysteries

"*SACRIFICE* is the best novel I've read this year. Not just the best mystery, but the best novel, period."
—Jeremiah Healy

## COMEBACK

"*Comeback* is so good, you want to sit down and read it all at once. It's got love and shame and money and the Minnesota woods and lakes, and dark mystery, and a reluctant hero, and it's written with humor and passion."
—Garrison Keillor

"[A] well-written, fast-reading thriller. . . . It's got everything."
—*Minneapolis St. Paul Magazine*

## SWING

"Solidly entertaining."
—ALA *Booklist*

"*Swing* has muscle. *Swing* has heart, too. . . . The plot twists as unpredictably as a hangman's rope. . . . Enger has created an amateur P.I. in a series to watch."
—*Alfred Hitchcock Mystery Magazine*

## STRIKE

"Compelling. . . ."
—*Publishers Weekly*

"Gun finds himself in the middle of intense racial politics, Indian land disputes, and a lot of good, old-fashioned danger."
—*The Prime Suspects*

**Books by L. L. Enger**

Comeback
Sacrifice
Strike
Swing

Published by POCKET BOOKS

A GUN PEDERSEN MYSTERY

# SACRIFICE

## L.L. ENGER

POCKET BOOKS

New York   London   Toronto   Sydney   Tokyo   Singapore

This book is a work of fiction. Names, characters, places and
incidents are either products of the author's imagination or are used
fictitiously. Any resemblance to actual events or locales or persons,
living or dead, is entirely coincidental.

An *Original* Publication of POCKET BOOKS

POCKET BOOKS, a division of Simon & Schuster Inc.
1230 Avenue of the Americas, New York, NY 10020

ISBN: 0-671-74482-8

First Pocket Books printing August 1993

10 9 8 7 6 5 4 3 2 1

POCKET and colophon are registered trademarks of
Simon & Schuster Inc.

Cover art by Stephen Peringer

Printed in the U.S.A.

*For Mom and Dad*

# SACRIFICE

*H*e thought of it so hard and often that the event ceased to be a reconstruction and became, almost, a memory. A memory that dried the tongue. Against logic, it was still the burial that bothered Gun the most.

Not the killing.

That part was horrible enough, true, it came to him like a familiar piece of silent film, black and white. The steady rain falling on the small town through the night. The June coolness rising in a mist from the earth as the drops spatter thick on the ballfield grass. The two men standing on the short-clipped grass in the rain.

Gun can't hear the men. He can't hear their words nor the solid maritime beat of the rain. But he sees their faces, indistinct from bad weather and emotion, and he sees the rigidity in their postures. They are arguing. He sees the shape and gleam of the object between them, but who holds it, he cannot tell.

Then one man—they are only shapes now, the rain

1

*is sweeping in so hard from Superior—one man shoves, and the other draws a hand backward, and the object swings in a silver stop-motion crescent. In Gun's mind it is what a shooting star would look like through a curtain of rain. And one man falls and stays fallen.*

*If it could only end there.*

*But it never does. Because the silent reel is over, and when the next one starts it has color and sound. The sound is mostly the spade hitting earth, and it changes texture as the grave gets deeper: The first blows are simple slaps of muck, then there is the soft solid give as the blade cuts clay. Gun sees the digger's legs, and they are covered with brown-black mud. He sees the ballfield with its proud-cut grass and the barren spot behind the visitors' dugout. He sees the face of the killed man, the sodden hair and earth-pressed cheek. The lower jaw distended, the head thrown back, a graceful haft of dark wood protruding upward from the red mouth like the handle in a sword-swallower's act.*

*A tall man wields the shovel. He handles the tool with a natural authority, lengthening the hole, stepping down in, working hard but not frantically as the rain continues to fall. He is a man, Gun knows, whose mind is not subject to change.*

*Now the digger pulls himself out from the pit and drops the tool. Next comes the bending down and the grasping of hands, the slow drag rippling through muck, the slack tumble that begins the patient wait.*

# 1

*T*hey waited for him every time he went home; it was like they could read his mind, or sense his car, or maybe smell him coming. Day or night, the whitetails didn't care—he'd be driving up 41, almost there and thinking, Ha, made it, and that's when some restless doe would sprint out from the trees and try her Olympic best to end up on his shirtfront. A few scares over the years, and also some venison, and he'd learned to slow down beyond the Michigan line. There was something suicidal about these Peninsula deer, and who could blame them? Average snowfall up here was 187 inches. Chop down through *that* with your dainty little hooves.

This year's doe waited until the hour before sunrise.

Gun Pedersen was at the wheel of a rented Dodge, getting closer to his home town every minute and hoping the Michigan herd had finally forgotten to send him a sacrifice. Then he saw her. She was a stringy little female, still showing her winter ribs though it was early May, and she stepped up out of the ditch and into the high beams well in front of the car. He had plenty of time. She stood there on the blacktop and swung her head to stare at him as he slowed, easy on the brakes because Carol Long was sleeping next to him, her cheek against his elbow. The doe looked sleepy, too, not moving as the car neared, only her ears fluttering forward and back. A clod of dirty snow stuck to her flank. He braked harder, and the back tires slid to the left and then caught again, and he smoothed the Dodge down to a walk, switched the beams to low. The doe blinked slowly. The car stopped with maybe five feet to go. The doe stayed.

"Mm. Are we there?" Carol opened her eyes. She was wrapped in a woolen Nez Percé blanket. She sat up, tightening it around her shoulders, and beheld the doe. "Oh. She looks lost." The doe was bobbing her head side to side.

"Well, we can't go through her. You want to chase her away, or should I?"

"We could turn around and go home," Carol said. She took a brush from her handbag on the dash and ran it through her hair, very businesslike. This trip hadn't been her idea.

Gun sighed through his nose and rapped the windshield with his knuckles. The doe lowered her head— she was a ropy one, mighty depressed—and came closer. Her eyes were empty as Ping-Pong balls. Carol said, "Poor girl. What a winter."

He opened the door then, and the doe's ears twitched hard, and at last some of the twitch came into her big empty eyes, and Gun stood from the car and smacked the hood with an open palm. She sprang back and stumbled, got to her feet and bounced away, her bright flag twirling.

Gun walked around the car, stretching. They had left Stony, Minnesota, the previous night, and Carol had been sullen all the way to Duluth, claiming thoughtfulness. He allowed there was enough to think about. He was thoughtful himself; driving to funerals will do that to you, especially funerals that are a quarter century late. He thought of poor Harry Summers, whose casket would be closed.

Carol stayed in the car. She rolled down her window and spoke to him through it. "How far to Copper Strike?"

"Half hour. You look good." Though not much of her was showing; it was too dark. You could see a little white at the corners of her eyes, a few jags of white in the black of her hair. Her teeth were there someplace, if she'd just smile.

"Is it cold, or is it me?" Carol said.

"It's you." It was, too. The Upper Peninsula was rarely this mild so soon in May, but he knew Carol Long wished to concentrate on warmer matters just now. A small and familiar ceremony, for one, with people they both knew. A bare blue-white Caribbean beach, and a cottage close to the water with linen curtains and unpainted boards, bleached as bone. A warm bedroom in the cottage, good champagne in a bottle sweating on the pillow.

"I'm sorry," she said. "I don't mean to be bitchy."

"It's lousy timing, that's all. The funeral's today. We'll rest up and go back tomorrow. Everyone will understand."

She put her hand to her forehead—he could see her fingers, pale as dawn. "It's too much to do. We're getting married in less than a week. We have reservations"—she paused, as if thinking how that sounded—"plans, and now this funeral, and it's a long, *long* drive, Gun."

He knew exactly what he should not say, but driving

all night and concentrating for whitetails had robbed him of restraint. "Carol, it's not so bad. Just think, you get to meet my folks."

She rolled up the window.

It was hardly stunning that Carol hadn't met the Pedersens, Madilyn and Gunsten Soren. Gun didn't get back that often; maybe every two years once he'd lost Amanda and then quit the Detroit Tigers back in '80. He hadn't called them much since then, either. His parents knew why Amanda had gotten on that plane, and they knew what had led up to it. Even here in the U.P. there were enough inquiring minds to warrant a rack of tabloids at the corner grocer's, and Gun hated his imagination for telling him how it must have been: his mother, Madilyn, pushing the wire cart through the checkout, her delicate shoes tapping the green linoleum as she glanced over the headlines, pretending to pick out a pack of chewing gum. And there it would be, just north of the Juicy Fruit, the lead story in the *World Spectator:* "Slugger Throws Out Wife, Slides in Safely with Starlet." Pictures Inside! And now Madilyn's cheeks go white, and her shoes go quiet as she pays for the paper, rolling it tightly so no one will see.

Amanda had seen that paper, too. The press had been after her, first the dirty rags and then the legitimate rags, and finally she'd boarded Flight 347 for Minnesota, where the Twins were hosting the Tigers. She was coming to talk to him, he knew, to blow up the righteous gale he deserved—and then, he hoped, to forgive him. Except the plane went down. It landed on its nose in a farmer's cornfield in Wisconsin, and no one lived. Some of the passengers had to be dug out of the ground before they could be put back in.

Carol said, "Gun, it's uncomfortable. Meeting

them. It's my second time around, and I don't know what to be."

He looked over at her and saw dawn breathing light on the east. He said, "Let's see. Not virginal, I guess."

No smile.

"They'll welcome you. Don't worry."

She sat still in her seat, upright now. His shoulder missed her heat. She said, "They're not even coming for the wedding. We asked them, and they're not coming. That's some welcome."

"You're reading them wrong, Carol."

"Whatever you say."

He tried saying nothing, but it didn't work. "Listen. I haven't included my folks in my life very much, not for a long time. It was—hard, for a while, with them."

She was quiet.

"I didn't live the way they live. I had some success, and it screwed me up and ended badly, and I regret that. It wasn't easy on them nor on me. Who knows what happens to us, why we become what we do? So now you and I have a happy event. Let's be glad about it, but don't be betting on the fatted calf. I'm sorry. Dad quit slapping me on the back a lot of years ago."

The world was turning to gray as they drove, a fine unhurried Michigan fog. Carol said, "We could've come later. I don't see the urgency of this funeral. This person, Harry—he died so long ago."

"He was nineteen," Gun said. "Back in 'sixty-nine. Got picked in the draft, and a few days later he disappeared. Copper Strike's a small town, and you can imagine the talk, Canada so close. He had a lot of family across the border, too. I think a lot of people expected him to jump. But he was a good kid." Gun thought a minute, trying to remember what he'd really known of Harry. He couldn't remember much. "Good family," he said. Those were his father's words, from the letter he'd sent the previous week.

*Remember Harry Summers? Good kid, good fami-
ly. Good shortstop also, you will recall. Well, they
were out digging foundations for the new school
here last week, and they found some bones. Guess
what, they were Harry's.*

"He was the kid everyone had big hopes for," Gun
said. "I didn't know him well, but he belonged to my
town. And he vanished, and we've all invested a lot of
years wondering where he is, or was, and now we
know. It just seemed right to come."

The Dodge passed a sign that said Copper Strike 5.
He shook his head and glanced at Carol, and there was
enough light now to show she hadn't been listening.

He said, "I guess something else's wrong."

She looked over, and he could make out the pure
underwater green of her eyes. The gentle lines at the
corners. She said, "I guess so. I guess I'm forty-two
years old, and I'm meeting your parents, and I'm
afraid they'll want Amanda back."

*No, no,* he should have said, *no one expects that. Not
them, and not me.* And this was true, Gun was
confident of it, but he held silent, uncertain of the
value of talk.

The fact was he had discussed Amanda's death with
his parents just once. It was two weeks after Amanda's
plane went down, one week after her funeral. He'd left
his daughter Mazy with friends and driven all morning through a steamy August rain. With less than a
mile to go the usual deer had bolted over the road, and
he'd steered straight for it, hitting the gas. The damn
thing had escaped, not serious about dying after all. In
his parents' kitchen he had told them to ask what
questions they would, and he had answered them
straight, face to face, letting them understand in
daylight which things about him were true and which

not true. In his mind he gave them permission to judge him, and in the end they had not. Nor had they tried to absolve him. Madilyn had said, "Will you keep Mazy with you?" which only raised doubts about whether he should.

Gunsten had raised himself wordlessly from a kitchen chair and walked outside into the soaking woods and not come back for four long days.

They ascended a gentle rise of smooth earth and pines where the road swept eastward around a sudden large upjut of black bedrock. The pines glistened with dark new spring. The road swung out to a clear leap where you could see Superior on uncloudy days, twelve miles east, the mouth of Keweenaw Bay, and then it turned north again and took them at last down into the extinct glory of the town of Copper Strike.

"My word," Carol said.

He looked at her.

"It's nineteen fifty-five here."

He nodded, faintly surprised. The ken of his childhood had scarcely changed except to age: the narrow houses leaning in close to the road with their slap-fitting doors and brick-patterned tar paper that had endured the seasons since Truman took office, or before. Most of these appeared empty, porches in ruin. There was the same gray of sky and the dark gray-brown of springtime muck. He felt he had first left Copper Strike on this same day, a day of no morning and no night, where time moved like a tortoise through the streets, leaving a gray-brown trail.

He heard Carol inhale and followed her eyes. The day's first sun was burning through fog. She was looking off to the right at a big roadside placard. It was a picture of Gun's own face, youthful and eminently faded, painted on boards now so old they were loose and peeling. In 1964 that sign had gone up, the year of

Gun's big-league debut. He'd lost Rookie of the Year to Tony Oliva, but not by much, and the Copper Strike High School art class had created this sign and unveiled it when he came home after the season. HOME OF GUN PEDERSEN, it said. A relic in his honor. It gave Gun an odd downturn in the stomach.

He pretended he hadn't seen it, and so did Carol.

They drove through town on its near-empty Main Street, the only cars those parked in front of the Lode Café.

"Breakfast?" Gun said.

"Let's just get there."

They got there as the last of the fog trailed off. The Pedersens lived on acreage a few miles north of town, and like the rest of Copper Strike the place had changed little. The house was of weathered wood that had never seen paint. The big basswoods all around had gotten bigger and completely hidden the several cabins out back they rented to summer people. The bare wood barn, Gunsten's workshop, leaned a little harder west. Lots of tulipy color around the buildings; Madilyn, by the looks of it, had gotten her bulbs out on time.

Gunsten Soren was on the porch. He had on gray woolen pants and a white cotton T-shirt. He stood there in the sun like it was a warm shower, his head tossed back, mouth slightly open. He had most of his son's six-feet-six. Not quite all of it. His white hair was as thick as Gun's but longer, abundant to the shoulders.

Carol said, "He looks like a prophet."

"Here we go," Gun said.

# 2

On the porch Gun said, "Carol, my dad." Gunsten stood to full height and held out a hand. Gun wondered how the old man looked to Carol up close; on the chilly side, he guessed. Gunsten had skin the color of red oak and a pair of stark, aggressive eyebrows that looked like white-capped waves. The eyes themselves were dark brown, not the Norwegian blue people expected. They weren't warm eyes. They appeared to reserve judgment—or, if they judged, to curtain the results.

"I'm Gunsten," the old man said. Carol shook the hand. He said, "Madilyn's got breakfast," and they went in.

She was a woman of gracious proportions, Madilyn, in her early seventies now but built trim, her hair a natural brown with not much more gray in it than Carol Long's. It was cut athletically short, which looked right with what she wore: a pair of tight-at-the-

11

ankle jeans that looked like two exclamation points joined at the head, Nikes, and a roomy gray sweatshirt. Her eyes had both the warmth and blue color her husband's lacked. "Gun! And Carol! Now sit you down, kids. Oh, I've made *way* too much food this morning—"

They had tart heavy-skinned grapefruit rescued by brown sugar, and soft-boiled eggs, and homemade doughnuts that Madilyn, from Virginia, called frycakes, and hot coffee brewed with chicory, a habit Gunsten had learned decades before from a Cajun copper miner, though he used cream in the coffee now, conceding an aging stomach. They had hash-browned potatoes fried crisp. They had venison sausage from Neb Summers, Copper Strike's police chief, who'd hit four deer so far in city automobiles but who never wasted the meat. Neb was Harry Summers's uncle.

"Ooh, boy." Gun sat back. Driving all night and now this meal—his strength had been sucked out and replaced by cholesterol. Also he felt regretful—having eaten, now they'd have to talk.

Gunsten said, "It's a pretty good day for a burial."

"How'd they find him, Dad?"

"It's not breakfast talk. Let it rest a bit." The old man was still good at this, bringing up a weighty subject and then dropping it when you lifted your end.

Madilyn said, "Carol, it was wonderful of you to come. I can imagine how it complicates your plans."

"Well," Carol said, but apparently it led her nowhere, and she let it hang.

"At least this way we get to meet you," Madilyn said. She smiled, saying it, and Gun recognized his mother's discomfort.

"I suppose," Carol said, "you could have met me at the wedding." She was smiling, too, sweet as cherry ice. Gun thought, Oh man.

Gunsten rose from the table. "I got a run to make. Mrs. Pernula needs a new windowsill back of her house, she'll be perky enough if I don't get to it. You want to come?"

It was directed at Gun, but Carol seized on it, still with the happy face. "I'd like that. We'll get acquainted on the job."

Gunsten shrugged with his whitecap brows. "Let's go, then," he said, and went out, Carol following. Going out the door, she fired a look at Gun that he could not decipher, though he suspected it was best not to try too hard.

"Carol is very sweet," Madilyn said, "and very nervous. I'm sorry she's unhappy."

They had washed and dried the breakfast dishes, old Currier and Ives blue-on-white plates Gun remembered from the big occasions of his youth. They went out and stood awkwardly on the porch until Madilyn mentioned a trellis that needed fixing. On the south side, where the morning glories were coming up.

"She doesn't know what's expected of her," Gun said. He had a nail between his fingers and two more in his teeth. One of his father's slender Brukker hammers was in his right hand.

"We meant no unkindness, not planning to come to your wedding. We meant to keep things comfortable for you."

The trellis wasn't in bad shape, just loose from the weight of wind and vines, but it was old wood that would split if not handled carefully. Gun tapped the sharp end of the nail to flatten it, then turned it around and drove it through an upper slat into the bare bark-colored siding of the house. The slat didn't split.

"It's not important, Mom."

"We want you to be happy, Gun. That's never changed."

His mother didn't sound old, or uncomfortable, either, now that they were alone. Just Mom, standing in her Nikes on the morning-glory loam.

He chose another slat, another nail. "Carol's afraid of something," he said. He hammered the nail home.

"What's that, son?"

He took the last nail, picked a final place where the trellis hung out from the wall, and, forgetting to flatten the point, began driving it in. He was thinking something he had not known a moment ago. A true surprise, like a stranger walking up behind you and then saying your name, giving you bad news.

"She's afraid to be married to me," he said, hammering, and the trellis stayed firm but the damn siding split beneath the nail.

Madilyn was quiet.

"Tell me about Harry," Gun said.

Madilyn had been in town the day of Harry's surprise exhumation. The Caterpillar was digging foundations for a new school. Copper Strike's old high school, built with mining money in 1914, had been falling down for years. Last spring some kids in junior high band had been practicing in the auditorium when the girl playing tuba squatted on a low note a little too long, and part of the ceiling drifted down, plaster snowing all over them. After this, and much local soul-searching and much chastising from the state education folks, the big day had come, and so had the Caterpillar.

"He was digging up the old ballfield, Gun, the one you played on. It's good high land, clay soil; that's where the new school will go. I saw the digging from a distance when I went into the Garden and Seed. But when I got done and stepped back out, there went the ambulance, *whoop!* Lights on and howling, up toward the ballfield. I thought sure the Caterpillar had turned over on its driver."

"You went up there?"

"Along with a few others. Very few, fifteen or so. This town has gotten pretty sorry."

Gun waited. His mother hesitated, then seemed to gather her story around her and went on.

"Henry Littenen was there. Off-duty, he was wearing jeans. It was right down at the ballfield. One of the dugouts had been tipped over on its roof, and there was a big mound of earth next to it. The Caterpillar was shut off, and the ambulance was pulled in close and shut off, too, and both drivers were talking to Henry. It was windy, you couldn't really hear them. You remember Hunter Watson."

Gun nodded. Watson was Copper Strike's remaining attorney. He had a police scanner on his desk but was rumored not to need it, his ear was that close to the ground.

"Hunter was there. I asked him what was happening, and he said there'd been some bones found. I think he'd heard it on his little set."

"Did they know it was Harry?"

Madilyn looked away. "At first they didn't even know it was human. Hunter said they had found—an arm, I think it was. The long bone. They speculated about beef and bear and everything else. But they kept going, and they found the rest."

"When did they realize who it was?"

"Folks guessed it pretty much right away. How many mysterious disappearances did we ever have in Copper Strike?"

Gun considered the question. "Well, some."

"None like Harry Summers's. Most of them, nobody missed."

"No." It was true. Gun could remember names,

Miller Habsburg, who had lived in a shack behind the old dance hall, and Barefoot Jupe Robins, and a few others who'd gone missing years before; but their faces were long gone, faded to dirt.

"The dental records proved it, of course. You're lucky not to have seen Neb after it turned out to be Harry. He loved that nephew of his. He was probably the last man in town who still believed Harry was alive somewhere."

"How's Neb doing?"

Madilyn looked at him closely. "Well. You knew he had cancer. A long time now."

"Yes."

"His city pension starts next fall. The council offered it to him some time back, when he first got sick, but he wouldn't take it. Insisted he'd earn the whole thing out, but of course he felt fairly good back then."

"He doesn't feel good now."

"No. But he's not going to the council to ask for any favors. He's willful, Neb Summers. Finally understanding that the cancer's tougher than Korea was. He's going to retire, and then he's going to die."

The Peninsula, Gun thought, was getting to be a melancholy place. "Good thing he's got Henry Littenen still," he said.

"Yes. Henry." But she was distracted now; something in the story she'd told was poking at her and hitting a soft spot. She put a hand on Gun's arm.

"What is it, Mom?"

"Oh, sweetie. It's just the horrible thing I saw, I can't seem to forget it."

He pulled her into his arms, Madilyn such a strong woman with all these years behind her, but now, suddenly, needing her son. He thought: At last, I am glad I came.

"I was watching, alongside Hunter, and suddenly he

pointed at the tipped-up dugout. On the mound of earth beside it. They'd put the bones there under some plastic, but the wind blew it aside, and we could see them. Gun? The bones were black."

"What?"

"I wouldn't have been afraid—it's foolish—but they were all dark. Like they were down in the ground too deep for too long, and all the paleness leached out of them." Her voice went quiet and brittle. "They lay there exposed and black. I saw one of the leg bones, and somehow the ankle had hung on, and the foot was still attached. All those little birdlike bones, the toes, and they were black and crooked, lying out in the air. And it wouldn't have scared me if they were white, like in pictures you see of the desert, but they were black; and Gun, I'm still afraid, and I don't even know why."

When the car drove up Gun and Madilyn were back in the house drinking coffee, Gun missing his tobacco and amazed that at his age he would not think of smoking in his mother's kitchen. They heard the car and looked at each other.

"I wonder how they got along," Madilyn said, but it wasn't Gunsten and Carol.

It was Henry Littenen. He was balding since Gun had seen him last, but he was in shape, five-ten with good high shoulders. His long, likable face was even longer because of the unfaithful hairline. He wasn't smiling. He was in uniform and carried a small corrugated cardboard box.

"Hank, good to see you. I understand you're still Neb's right hand." Gun stood, shook, pulled out a chair. Henry sat.

"More like both hands now. Gun, damn it, I wisht I had a happier reason for coming out here. I didn't see your dad's truck in the yard."

"Nope. Want coffee?"

"It's sort of urgent. Can you tell me where he is?"

"Mrs. Pernula's," Madilyn said. "He's putting in a sill."

Gun said, "He'll be straight back. What's the rush?"

Henry's eyes turned a worried shade. He laid the cardboard box on the table. "Look then, if you want."

Gun picked it up. The box was a cube of perhaps four inches. It was so light and dry he could barely feel it in his fingers. He eased the lid open. There was a thin layer of dirt across the bottom, dust really, and a key ring holding a pair of keys. It was the key ring that mattered.

"Where'd you find this?" Gun said.

"I only saw but one ring like that one," Henry said.

"Me, too." It was a heavy ring, big around as a silver dollar, and it gleamed obsidian black, shiny as water in the bottom of the box. Its tips, the ends that you pried up to put a new key on or take one off, were plated gold.

"Where'd you get it?" Gun said again. He had given the ring, and the keys upon it, and all that those keys opened, to his father. Years ago. About the time the HOME OF . . . sign went up.

"Aw, hell, Gun," Henry said. "I don't know what it means. But when we dug up old Harry's bones, these keys—they came up too."

# 3

Of course they're mine." Gunsten and Carol had returned not five minutes after Henry capitulated and accepted coffee. "You should know that, Hank. They been lost so long I stopped thinking about 'em. Lost as a lawyer's soul. Where'd *you* find 'em?" He was holding the prodigal key ring in his palm and looking at Littenen like he could see straight through to the back of his head.

"Gunsten, I'm sorry, but they came up with Harry Summers."

It seemed to puzzle the old man at first. His head cocked like a listening spaniel's, white eyebrows knocking together.

"I mean, when we dug him up—" Henry started. Gun remembered this about Henry, he was fine until he got nervous and then he turned into an explainer.

"I heard you," Gunsten said, and beneath his breath: "Well, I'm blasted."

"Something I ought to know, Gunsten?" Henry offered.

"You're a good man, Henry," Gunsten said. "So shut up now while I think."

Gun's father had the gift of directness.

In the quiet that surrounded the old man's thinking Gun looked at Carol, who hadn't even sat down yet. She stood at the kitchen door, the sun haloing in around her and teasing up her hair. Light so direct, Gun suddenly realized, was kind to Carol Long in ways it wasn't to most women her age; her straight, disciplined chin invited close inspection, along with her crested cheekbones, her sheer swept brows. In the utopian sun Carol's hair was black, the occasional grays struck to white. He felt a pull toward her. It was good to feel, after recent days. But she wasn't looking back at him. Her mouth was set and unreadable. Her green eyes were strong as a workman's clamp. She was looking at Gun's father, who stood in the space between them. She was watching Gunsten think.

"Do these put me in a little warm water?" Gunsten said finally, jingling keys at Henry.

Henry wouldn't commit. "It's a curious circumstance, is what it is."

"And who knows of it?"

Madilyn said, "Gunsten?"

"I know," Henry said. He hesitated. 'Yes, Neb knows. And I volunteered to come talk to you. Neb's getting sadder all the time, he's lost Harry all over again. He didn't need this."

Gun said, "What are you talking about?"

"Come on, Gun, don't make this hard on me." Henry stood up now, his feet scuffing like those of an unwelcome man. "Neb and your dad've been friends a long time. Since before Harry died, way before. So now the poor kid comes back, only he's bones, and

20

what's he carrying but this key ring? I'm sorry," he said, looking up into Gunsten's face, "but you can see how it makes Neb wonder."

"Wonder what?" Gun said. "So what if Harry had those keys? I remember they spent some time in *your* pocket once."

Littenen didn't blush at that, just made his feet still on the linoleum and looked at the old man. Gunsten's gaze was steady, aimed downhill at Henry, and Gun remembered how intimidating it could be. Finally Henry said, his batteries getting low, "Gunsten, please. If you know how Harry came to die with that key ring on his person, then I sure hope you'll decide to tell me about it. You don't, I'm awful sorry to say it, but there's bound to be some warmth over the whole affair. You planning on going to the memorial service today?"

"We are," Gunsten said.

"I wouldn't," Henry returned. "On account of Neb's boy Calvin. He's a brooder, like you didn't know it. He's already thinking you murdered his cousin Harry."

Carol entered the talk at last. "I thought only you and Neb knew about the key ring."

Henry looked at her for the first time, seemed caught by the green eyes and looked away. "Well, now, Neb's grieving, you see. And Cal is, too. Those bones are sorrow enough for most of us here, but for a Summers they're *family*. Can't a family talk?"

Gun saw the sternness go out of his father's eyes then and quiet humor enter them. "Calvin believes *I* killed him?"

Madilyn was staying quiet, but Gun noticed fear at the corners of her mouth. It was the second time today he'd seen that; third time in his life.

"He does, so says Neb. Now, Neb believes no such

21

thing; but he'd rather you stayed home today, you folks. Calvin's a spooky sort of piss-ant—I'm sorry, Madilyn."

She seemed not to hear him.

Gun himself felt little regret at the prospect of missing Harry's funeral. The drive notwithstanding, he felt almost glad to have the excuse. It was one thing to honor the memory of youth wasted and long-grieved, but the keys changed things. They turned it quickly and viciously personal. It was, he thought, as if you were sitting silently in the back row at a church of comfort, the message spreading gentle on your wounds, only to have the preacher break off his words suddenly and point his long finger straight at your unprepared heart: *Sinner!* But it was Gun's father being summoned, and it made Gun more uneasy than if it had been himself.

"Hank," Gunsten said, "you've filled your obligation. Now you go home and change, and I expect we'll see you at the service."

Madilyn had her eyes shut. Carol's were like two disbelieving moons.

Henry said, "Please, sir. Neb and you were always friendly. Won't you consider him?"

"It's for Neb I'm going. Calvin's the one I won't consider."

Gun told himself: Don't talk. It's still the old man's house. He glanced at Carol and saw she was watching him intently now.

Henry set his cup down on the table. It was three quarters full. "You'll hurt an old friend. He's dying, too."

"I'm truly sorry. But it's his son that's hurting him. Neb would want me there. Scared of his own unbalanced son," Gunsten said, nailing the adjective. "You think I'm going to bend for that?"

# 4

$L$et him go to the service then," Carol said. "I don't see why *you* have to."

They were alone in the kitchen. Henry had driven away with his long face stretched, and Gun's folks had wandered outside, deep in voiceless discussion. The sun had let off through the east windows and was just starting to hit the southern exposure, bouncing off the new basswood leaves and bringing their soft odor inside.

"Now you've seen my dad," Gun said.

"You feel like you have to keep him out of trouble?"

Gun wondered about it for a moment and couldn't decide. "I don't think so. Maybe I want to keep Cal Summers out of trouble."

"Gun, those keys—what do they open?"

"They're a set to a boathouse and lake cabin over on Keweenaw Bay. My dad had always wanted a place over there, with a big wooden boat he could drive around. I bought it for him and Mom after my second season with the Tigers. I picked out that key ring special, thought it was elegant."

"Pretty sweet. Do *you* know why Harry had them when he died?"

"Dad would let people use the place occasionally, if it was someone he liked. He liked Hank Littenen enough to let him take Jeannie there for their honeymoon."

"Will he talk to you about it?"

"Not if he doesn't want to."

She'd been giving him those green lamps of hers with the frost full-tilt but smiled now in a whipped way and said, "Well, great. You'd better get ready if you're going to that service. I'm staying here. Do you realize we haven't even taken our suitcases out of the car? This is going even better than expected."

She went out to get the luggage, and he sat at the kitchen table and let her do it.

The service was held outdoors in a semicircle of warm sun behind the redstone Presbyterian church. The perimeter was shut in cool shadow by a sickle-shaped grove of thick white pines, tall virgins that had escaped the loggers. It was said that Max Saupuna, the founder of Copper Strike in 1887 and a Lutheran Finn, had ordered that the trees be spared when the builders broke ground for the church; three years later Saupuna was gone, lying in a hammock in Mexico City in a new mansion built with copper money. The trees remained. The town library still had dispatches Max had sent to the local paper, the *Miner,* lauding life among the happy Aztecs.

The minister was a woman with wide white robes and a cheeky face full of perspiration and self-esteem.

She shook Gun's hand with a firm grip and told him, "Welcome back," though he had never seen her before and there was a novelty about her that made it clear Copper Strike was not her town.

"Thank you."

"Did you know Mr. Summers?"

"Not well." Just well enough to understand that he'd never been called Mr. Summers.

"It was good of you to come. Hel-*lo*, Madilyn, Gunsten."

Gun got away and found three unoccupied folding chairs near the back. The heat was a little astonishing for May, in the low seventies, and he removed his light-gray suit jacket and laid it across the chairs to reserve them. No one was sitting down yet, and the little clearing was getting crowded. And noisy. It came to him that Harry Summers was responsible for two of the most momentous events here in a quarter century: getting lost, and getting found again.

"Gun? It took *this* to bring you back?"

The voice made a familiar sweet splash, like the first cold melon of a long August. He said, "Hanna," and he turned.

Hanna Donnell was the first girl Gun had seriously pursued when at seventeen it became clear he might indeed have the chance to whack baseballs for a living. She stood before him now, same bright hair like orange-blossom honey, though it was cut shorter, just touching her shoulders. Same laughing smile, too; it had frustrated him then, when he didn't want to feel like her favorite cousin, but he could afford it now. It felt fine.

"I thought you might be back for Harry," she said.

"Hanna. You look good, the adult version."

She laughed. "I get my exercise, and I've stopped doing chocolate. You never wrote to me."

"I've never been good at keeping up. Ask my folks."

"Oh, I've kept up with *you*, though. You went to the Tigers, and I started reading box scores. My husband got a huge kick out of that, thought I was fantasizing. Not a jealous bone, he's a sweetie."

Gun wondered if he was supposed to reply to that, but Hanna went on. "We got to some games even, down to Tiger Stadium. Was *that* strange, looking down from that left-field deck, watching you roam the outfield. Seeing you and knowing you couldn't see me."

Overhead the white pines brushed together in a slow sway, their branches and fine soft needles warning of gusts to come. Gun couldn't feel it yet but guessed that the giddy spring warmth would be knocked on its backside before long. He said, "You mentioned a husband?"

"Steven. He's not much for baseball. We used to sit right down by the railing on the second deck."

Something changed in her expression as she talked. The light that had been reflected so sweetly from her cheekbones dulled, and her face itself lost some of its tart-apple roundness; the slight lines around her mouth deepened to wrinkles.

"Second deck was what we could afford," she said.

Gun lacked words.

"Oh, but we didn't come often. Three or four times a year." She laughed the hurt laugh of a high school girl. "'Course I could have had a season ticket every year you played, and you wouldn't have seen me up there." It was as if the words had been boxed in the basement too long and now were coming out into the daylight wrinkled and smelling of mold. She seemed to feel their wrongness, and it showed in the sudden dryness of her skin beneath the eyes, the tightwire of her upper lip.

He said, "Are you staying in town?"

"I didn't leave ever," Hanna said.

Above them the pine tops moved against the sky, bending one way and then another, sweeping for rainclouds. Gun watched Hanna in silence while she slipped a red vinyl purse from her arm and scuffled through it for Kleenex. Talk was surfacing in pockets around them as people drifted to folding chairs.

"I'm sorry, Gun. Maybe I'll see you before you leave."

"I'd like that," he told her. He meant it, but her eyes were still troubled as she left him, picking her way through folding chairs and marginal conversations.

The memorial service, it turned out, was so called because there was no body present and no casket, so memory was heavily relied upon to bring the deceased to the front of attention. There was a podium, with a microphone affixed to a stand with silver duct tape, and next to the podium a short cherry-stained table topped with a spray of spring flowers. Easter flowers, Gun thought, bright lilies and snapdragons and white-petal daisies. Perhaps four hundred people had accumulated in the churchyard. Many looked like people Gun had known, though their names bobbed just beyond reach. Neb Summers wasn't in sight, nor his son. Gun thought he saw Harry's parents, Myron and Nora Summers, but there was activity around them, and he couldn't be sure. Clara, the minister, went shiny-faced to the podium and tapped the tinny microphone.

"Welcome, everyone. I'm glad you came. The occasion is one I wish I could live up to. But the fact is, I've only lived in Copper Strike for two years, and of course I don't have any memories of Harry Summers. It would be unfair of me to eulogize him."

The wind was getting through the lower pines now and luffing at the edges of Clara's robes. To Gun's left Madilyn sat in a white-belted navy dress and onyx brooch, then Gunsten, tall and jagged, a beardless Moses in a brown wool suit.

Clara said, "So I'm going to leave the eulogies to you people today. Harry Summers has family here, and good friends. People who know that Harry's tragedy was made all the greater by his promise." She paused, and now through the crowd Gun found Neb and Calvin, seated rightly in the front row, and understood why he'd not recognized them sooner. He'd last seen Neb before the cancer struck, when the old cop still had weight and hair.

"I'm going to read from the Bible now, and then I'd like to depend for the rest of the service on your own memories of Harry. Just come on up. All right." She opened a Bible, its thin pages thup-thupping against the microphone as she sought the place.

She read from Lamentations, the book of sorrow, with a voice clean and husky. Gun did not remember the verses, but they were good: forthright words of grief and redemption, the kind usually heard least when needed most.

> *My enemies without cause hunted me down,*
> *They have silenced me in the pit*
> *and placed a stone on me. . . .*
> *I called on thy name, O Lord,*
> *Out of the lowest pit.*

Beneath Clara's voice the pines tossed with a noise like swelling surf. Neb Summers's head in the front row was held high, scalp dull under spidery hair; on his right Calvin's round head was bowed and quivering. The coolness that had entered the breeze, almost

28

as a relief, was suddenly more pronounced. Gun laid an arm across Madilyn's shoulders.

Clara read:

> *Thou didst draw near when I called on Thee;*
> *Thou didst say, "Do not fear!"*
> *O Lord, Thou didst plead my soul's cause;*
> *Thou hast redeemed my life.*

She closed her Bible. Gun closed his eyes in the quiet. He was at the Copper Strike high school ballpark in the autumn of 1968. It was the year the Tigers had taken it all, and afterward Gun had escaped the World Series crush with his family, brought Amanda and little Mazy up to the lake. They'd come to fish and hide out in the Indian summer but had stopped in Copper Strike to see Gun's parents. They told him then about the kid who'd been hanging around lately, the high school shortstop who'd taken Gun as his mentor. Harry Summers, nephew of Neb. "A decent boy, and he's got a good pick out there," his father had said. "Pretty swing as well. Make the kid's life, Mr. MVP. Give him a call."

So they'd gone out to the ballpark, just Harry and Gun, on a day long after the gold in the October trees had shriveled to brown and dropped away. Windbreaker weather, where the glove feels a little stiff against the palm until it gets some work. And work it got. Harry Summers was a shy, strong pup who looked laced up out of timber and leather, but he had more grace in those long limbs than it first appeared. He avoided Gun's eyes, avoided speech. They played some catch—first short, then long, the ball coming into Gun's glove with real snap even at fifty, sixty yards—then Gun opened his duffel bag and took out the bat. A thirty-five-inch H & B, pine tar generous on the handle and dark bruises up on the sweet spot from a week's happy hitting. In Game Seven he'd smoked one with this bat, his best connect of the Series, not even feeling it, and the ball had moaned away on a straight razor line and struck the fence in right-center half a foot from the ground. Now he stepped to the plate and pointed the bat between second and third. Harry grinned, his face a ripe peach, and crouched at shortstop. Gun tossed the ball up and swung, sending the kid a gentle bouncer. Harry scooped it up, saw Gun standing at the plate, bat cocked, and lobbed it carefully in. Gun had to reach behind himself to catch it barehanded. He called out, "Don't hurt me," and he saw Harry Summers laugh, the boy in glory now and beaming. He hit the kid a hard one this time, and Harry ranged off far to his left and shoehorned it smooth as licorice candy, set himself, fired a strike to Gun. Gun turned it into a line drive back to Harry's belt buckle. Easy. Then a grass-burner just off of third. Then a one-hopper deep in the hole. Harry couldn't miss.

He dreamed that way through Clara's prayer, then through a half dozen willing speakers who offered whatever fond or indulgent or stiff-chinned perspectives they felt were needed. It felt good to be disconnected in that way and Gun fought the inevitable return, but the afternoon's warmth had begun suddenly to deteroriate, and the service was winding down. In the front row Calvin Summers appeared to have his index finger buried knuckle-deep in his right ear. Gun recalled his father's assessment, *unbalanced,* and thought: Well, that'll do it.

There was a final prayer, and Clara dismissed. The wind was cold; Madilyn wore Gun's jacket on her shoulders, and Gun felt his own throat going mildly raw. He wondered idly why Neb and Calvin had chosen not to speak—though maybe they had and he'd missed them, gone in that dream. Even without them Harry Summers had been resurrected in such pale, tragic light that Gun found himself wondering if the boy had ever uttered a foul word or an errant statement; if he'd ever witnessed, say, the humiliation of a less-popular classmate and stood by and let it happen.

Of course he had. And of course it wasn't the sort of thing you remembered out loud at a funeral, nor should you. Now Gun realized something else: In the bright paradise of eulogy no one except Clara had even alluded to the fact that Harry was murdered. Again, it was only appropriate to show some regard for the family. He was sure Carol would say so. But as the people rose from their folding chairs, the wind making them tuck in their elbows and smile short good-byes at one another, Gun suspected another motive for such unanimous sentiment. He suspected that his hometown, like most others, had a preference for the status quo: that Harry's disappearance, unpleasant though it was, had early on become a part of the long lore of Copper Strike, Michigan; and that his abrupt unearthing would now be hurriedly woven into that history, with only superficial emphasis on the questions it raised. For now, yes, the killer and his reasons were a beguiling conversation piece. But without a quick—and mighty unlikely—resolution, Gun supposed the Harry Summers murder would cool into legend. After all, what small town didn't have its sordid, unsolved incident? And what town didn't come to wear it with some unspoken pride, like a henpecked man with a lovely mistress?

They were among the last to leave the churchyard. Gun waited in a spot of sun next to the west wall of the church while his mother spoke with long-missed friends and his father maintained a tall silence. Myron Summers and his wife Mavis, Harry's parents, moved through the assembled with stiff claspings and nods, as if grief was a disease of the joints. Mavis was black-veiled, the first such that Gun had ever seen outside of the movies, and a young man at her elbow shared some rough-shaped Summers features: the long, free limbs that looked fashioned at someone's workbench. He wore a respectful suit jacket over pressed olive chinos, but his headful of brown wire had lost its patience a long time ago and sprang forward, leading the way. Gun leaned against the red church brick and watched the young man pressing Mavis forward. The wall felt good at his back, full of sun. When Madilyn and Gunsten showed up, ready to go at last, he nearly hated to leave its comfort, the brick back there like the warmth of God.

Neb and Calvin Summers were standing on the pockmarked sidewalk in front of the church. Even stooped, Neb had his son by two or more inches, but the old man's disease had taken his color until he seemed barely visible, a tall, skinny length of bad health, fragile as a November cattail. Calvin still looked much as he had in junior high school, when Gun had last glimpsed him just before leaving for the minor leagues. Too big around for his height, too big for his delicate upturned cowboy boots. And too big to wear bright clothes. He wore a pink shirt as glossy as a grapefruit under a brown western-stitched jacket. His hands were impatient knots inside his pants pockets. He smelled a little like saddle soap and a lot like Vitalis.

"Hello, Neb. A good service," Gunsten said.

Neb's Adam's apple moved, but his voice seemed to

have stayed home in bed. Around them the last groups from the memorial service were breaking up and heading for their cars, the women's heels tapping on the sidewalk.

"The hell now, Dad," Calvin said. "I didn't guess old Pederson would come."

Gunsten let it go by. "Quite a crowd. Your nephew was a boy to be proud of."

"Yeah." Neb's voice came out low but surprisingly firm, and hearing it seemed to give him confidence. "Miss him like hell, me and Calvin. We ought be buryin' him now. Have to wait."

"Why is that?"

"Don't let's talk of that yet, Gunsten. Come to my office, maybe Monday. That's soon enough."

His father nodded, and Gun understood. Neb wanted to talk about the keys. Well, fine. Gun himself had been putting off thoughts of the keys until a chance should come to corner his dad about it. Which wouldn't be easy, because Carol was accurate about this: Gunsten *was* a prophet in some ways. He had a prophet's conviction in his own rightness, and a strength of will that often made true his predictions for the world at hand. If Gunsten had a reason for not talking, it would take more than a son or a sick old friend to change his mind.

"Naw, Dad, let's talk it over now," Calvin said. He had a loud voice, blind to proximity. "I don't *wanna* wait. All that time at the service we set there, and me thinking about those keys of Pedersen's, and now he shows up, the god*damned* arrogance—"

"Son," Neb said, but it was like stuffing the red hanky back in one's pocket with the bull already thundering down. "Son, *think.*" He coughed and laid a hand on Calvin's shoulder, a gesture half restraint and half for support.

"I thought already." Calvin slapped Neb's hand away like a horsefly, and Neb lost equilibrium. He fell forward, his knees buckling and hitting the sidewalk, the sound brittle as bamboo. Breath seemed to leave him, and he splayed his hands on the cement, holding the deck. Gun saw Calvin turn and look down at Neb Summers for long seconds. Neb's head was down and his shoulders shook and the two cords of skin up the back of his neck were white in the weakening sun.

Calvin's face showed nothing. He didn't speak or bend to assist. Instead Gunsten got down and steadied Neb, then motioned for Gun. The two of them eased the old cop upright and walked with him half a block to a big blue Pontiac. "I'm still drivin', though," Neb said. His right hand clawed in his pocket for keys. "It's some pathetic way to go, ain't it, boys?"

"I'll stop in Monday, Neb."

They were headed back toward the church when Neb called, huskily, "Send Cal over here, will ya? He needs a ride home." Gunsten nodded without looking back. Calvin watched them balefully as they approached, his fingers tugging at the too-short sleeves of his jacket. Gun felt his father's eyes catch and hold Calvin's, sensed at once the younger man's agitation, his discomfort with the silence between them. As they drew up Calvin smiled uneasily, swayed, and uttered exactly the wrong words: "Hey, I'm sorry. You believe it? He's a goddamned invalid now." And Gunsten drew back his open right hand, wide as a clump of dry sod, and swung it in a purposeful curve that took Calvin hard just below the left earlobe. Calvin made a half turn as he fell. He landed on his side with his knees crossed. Madilyn watched from the church steps, her face not frightened this time but set stiff as plaster. Gunsten nodded to her. He stepped over

Calvin, and Gun heard his low growl. "Get up now, run along. Your daddy's waitin'."

Then Gunsten reached Madilyn and tenderly took her hand while Calvin's head made drowsy movements and Vitalis shone in glassy dark spatters on the sidewalk.

# 5

*T*he doomed Copper Strike school had been built in 1908 one block past the last storefront on Main Street, so that a traveler standing at the four-way downtown could look west and see solid evidence that here was a city that had staked itself to the earth and intended to remain. It was a square three-story school of dark brown brick, with red stones mortised around the tall rectangular windows. Orange and purple and yellow cutouts of tulips hung in the windows of the lower grades. Over on the junior high side some kid had used blue spray paint to write CLASS MY ASS, '98 SUCKS on the cement steps leading into the gymnasium. The world, Gun thought, was concluding itself, but the yard was greening up nicely even so and was in fact still overhung with the unpruned arms of elm trees he remembered playing beneath. A small black dog, white-muzzle old, lay asleep next to an empty silver bike rack. Gun could hear the flag rope tinging against the steel pole in the center of the yard, but it was Saturday and no flag flew.

Gun had spent twelve years at this place, and it looked old, all right, but it really didn't look bad. Not like a building that had outlived its purpose and started shaking pieces of itself down on noisy children. He thought: Why tear it down?

But it was in Gun's nature to disbelieve the rule of time, and he knew it. It was why he'd been having his best season yet with the Tigers when he quit at the age of thirty-six. It was why, even now, he looked every day into the mirror over his bathroom sink, his jaw red from shaving and a cold-water rinse, and told himself, It's okay, you're not falling down yet, not even close—and then went out into his kitchen and down to the floor for pushups, ninety-six of them now, followed by three sets of crunches that flattened the gut into so many rolls of quarters. Because your best complaints against the rule of time were discipline and work. You were careful about your commitments, and you honored the ones you made, and you kept the bricks in place another day.

The two front doors were locked, but the side entrance to the gymnasium was blocked open a few inches by a white Reebok gymn bag. Gun wasn't in a hurry—his folks had gone home in their big square Buick—so he swung the door wide and entered. He was standing immediately next to the basketball floor, down in the concrete pit where the band played during games. Back from the pit rose what had once seemed a stadium-sized gallery of brown wooden seats—all empty today, all folded up tight, the aisles swept between them. A kid—no, he was a young man—was standing back of the free throw line. Top of the key, bouncing a dark leather basketball, his eyes diligent on the hoop. If he noticed Gun, he paid no mind. He was close to six feet, balding, and had a puffed, marshy face, as if he'd only recently gained weight after a slender boyhood. He was wearing tan custodian's khakis, and behind him a wide long-handled broom was propped against a square steel cage full of basketballs. Gun watched, sensing the young man's sudden self-consciousness as he set himself and shot. There wasn't enough wrist in it, and the ball bumped off the front of the rim.

Gun poked his hands down into his pockets.

The youthful janitor glanced at him briefly and flipped another ball up out of the cage. He bounced it twice and then shot without setting up, and it arced and descended, true as a cannonball this time, not touching the rim but almost ripping away the net.

"Two," Gun said.

"Three," said the janitor. He reached for another ball.

Gun watched him shoot a while. It was pleasant, hearing the sounds, the hollow auditorium belting back echoes of ball against floor, against backboard, against thrumming steel rim. And the kid—well, he *was* a kid, you got to be Gun's age and you could think so if you chose to—the kid was a decent shot. He stayed at the top of the key and pounded those leathers into the hoop, one after another. He emptied the cage, missing only three. A kid who liked an audience.

When he was done and slowly crisscrossing the gym floor scooping up balls he looked less like a boy and more like a janitor, and a question occurred to Gun. "Say. Did Green finally retire?" Green Tokannah, the eternal custodian of Copper Strike High School. The alpha and the omega.

"No, sir. Green's my supervisor, it's his last year. He gave me Saturdays 'cause I asked for 'em." An armload of basketballs thumped into the cage.

"Good judgment. Do you keep the grounds, too, or just work in the school?"

"Grounds're my main job, come summer. Green likes to stay out of the sun."

Gun stood in the band pit on the cool concrete, the chill of it like spring earth in the soles of his tennis shoes. Beneath the smells of dust and much-diluted soap was another, that of the enthusiastic sweat of children. He said, "So when's the wrecking party?"

"Next month. Does it smart a little?" The janitor spoke with a kindness Gun didn't expect, and in his rounded face Gun espied a kid who'd walked on these boards in a cap and gown not long ago, whose parents had probably snapped Instamatics of him from as close as these wooden seats allowed.

"Yes."

"Yeah. Well, the new one, they say it'll be good. There's gonna be a weight room, everything. A library with computers in it, TVs in every classroom."

"Sounds nice."

"'Course it'll be smaller, too. All this stuff for a town that's about dead. I don't know." The janitor loaded the last ball into the cage and picked up the broom, eyeing the black bristles.

"Did you happen to be here the day they found Harry Summers down at the ballyard?" Gun asked.

"Wish I'd'a been. Something real happening in Copper Strike, unbelievable, man. I'd like to have seen that. I was in Houghton, though, taking a long weekend. Some guys I know at the college, they're on the basketball team."

Gun nodded, lifted a hand. It was time to head back to his parents' house. There were the keys to be discussed with Gunsten and Madilyn, and a smile might be won from Carol.

The kid said, "The school got hold of me, though,

39

right off. Had to fill in for Green. He took it pretty bad, about that Summers. You probably know how bad news does to him."

Gun knew. Green's reaction to even mediocre news had always been to head for his stool in the Sidewalks Tavern, and once there not to rise from it until those who had brought the news, or were featured in it, disappeared from sight like folks sinking to the bottom of an amber lake.

"Yup. Guess I'll mosey. Good talking with you."

The janitor had rested his broom back against the cage and now held another basketball. He'd asked for Saturdays and they were a good day to work. Suddenly he said, "Say. Wait just a second, will you?" He jogged across the floor, his feet making light squeals on the boards. The exertion raised some pink in his face. He pulled a wallet from his khaki pants and shuffled through it, came up finally with a white card that he handed to Gun. It said COPPER STRIKE VIDEO, RENT ONE TODAY!

"Could you sign the back of it for me?" the janitor said. "Or wait, for my son. Five years old. He loves baseball."

By divine grace there was a pen in Gun's suit jacket. "What's his name?"

"Ace. Thanks."

Gun propped the card on his knee and wrote: *To Ace, son of the best shot I ever saw from the top of the key. Gun Pedersen.* Signing it, he noticed how the skin on the backs of his hands was beginning to change, the brown pigment separating into shapes like ragged new continents over the familiar tendons and veins.

# 6

He considered hiking down across the grounds to the torn-up baseball field, site of his earliest glory days and Harry's long purgatory, but both thoughts saddened him and he went instead to the car. Heading down Main he noticed two things: the fuel gauge, which read Empty, and a neon-green pickup in the rearview. It turned onto the street a ways behind him and then scooted up fast, cozying up to the bumper of the Dodge in a way that tightened Gun's grip on the shift knob. Gun checked his speed. Twenty-five, about all you wanted to do through an eight-block downtown, but the pickup back there was impatient. It sat way up high on a bad-ass four-wheel-drive chassis, the grille eating up Gun's mirror. Music thumped from it, guys in some loser metalhead group screaming out their anger over having been born ungifted. Gun slowed to twenty. The truck, unbelievably, got closer. He couldn't see the driver, the front end loomed so high, but he could see the plastic bug shield atop the grille. All these muscle trucks had the shields, and their owners painted slogans on them to show what men they were. This one said ANY TIME ANY PLACE.

Main Street was coming to end. Gun didn't want it to and didn't let himself wonder why. He slowed to fifteen. *You feeling irritated, buddy?* he thought. *Good.* The truck closed on him, music pounding like a surprised artery, the grille rocking with impatience. Gun felt the muscles stiffen around his backbone and something deep in his gut jell and lift like a cool chrome bubble. Then the passing storefronts gave way to a couple of gas stations, and Main petered out into plain county highway, speed limit fifty-five. The Dodge was on Empty. Disappointment hit Gun like a toothache. He'd have to stop for gas now, and the truck would honk and pass, the driver would lift a finger and be gone into greater Michigan.

He turned into the Conoco station on the right, the last pump going out of Copper Strike. He suddenly felt old and creaky, parking the Dodge in front of the self-serve island, and then his ears noticed that the music from the muscle truck hadn't gone away.

It had pulled in behind him.

The driver was already out of the cab, grabbing a hose of unleaded and giving Gun a prominent stare.

Gun stood from the Dodge. The guy looked thirty and aching to be eighteen. He had beached-blond hair gone long in back and cut to a casual standup on top. He was big—not more than six feet, but built like his Chevy, with barbell arms and a wide gorilla neck. His face was bad-stud handsome, with close-set brown eyes and heavy brows and the kind of tan you bought in the back of a beauty shop.

Apeneck regarded Gun with adequate cool. He

leaned into the cab and turned down the music. "Slow day, big guy?"

"Ah, the usual," Gun said mildly. The creaky feeling was long gone.

The guy lifted his upper lip to snicker.

Two girls came out of the Conoco station holding bags of chips. Eleven years old, no more, both wearing billowy nylon jackets with sleeves that reached to their fingertips. Eleven, a good age. A few more years and they'd never touch a potato chip again.

Apeneck's pump clicked off. He straightened, and Gun noticed his T-shirt. Light tan with big block letters:

## UN
## FUCKIN
## BELIEVABLE

The two girls, one a little taller and heavier than the other, were coming toward them. The shorter one had hair loosely bound in a ponytail and wore shorts cut off just above the knee.

"Hey, buddy," Gun called, "what's your name?"

"Dandrie," the guy said, but he wasn't looking at Gun. He was watching the girls. The taller one looked to have sneaked her mother's lipstick and was talking giggly about Ryan somebody, who was cute. They were coming toward Dandrie and he was looking them over, his shirt like an obscene billboard.

"Dandrie," Gun told him, "turn around."

"What?" Disbelief, and a shift of the simian shoulders.

"Face the truck," Gun said. He kept his voice down; didn't want the creep getting ugly in front of two little kids.

"The hell—" Dandrie snorted, but then he heard

the girls kidding each other, and his face got cool again and he called out, "Hey kids!" Still looking at Gun as he said it.

The girls looked up at the man's handsome face. They were smiling, attention being paid them by this really awesome big guy.

Gun started for the truck, not too fast. Forty feet to Dandrie, who was talking now. "Listen, can you sweethearts read this shirt?" He expanded his chest, and the words bloomed large. "Do you like it? 'Un-fuckin-believable.' What do you think it's talkin' about?" He glanced back to Gun and opened his mouth in a silent guffaw.

The taller girl's smile was the first to go. She could read all right but it was plain she didn't get it, didn't know why some guy in a green truck would want to come by and tell her a dirty word. Her confusion spread to the face of her friend.

Gun said, "Go home now, kids. Don't stay here." He kept walking. Twenty feet. The chrome bubble rose in his gut.

"That's right, sweethearts, go on now. But you come back in five, six years, I'll answer every question you got." Dandrie laughed and jogged his crotch with one hand. "Bye-bye. Bye-bye, babies."

But the girls were too snared in the moment to understand it was time to leave. They stood in uneasy fascination, like bystanders at an intersection where all the stoplights have malfunctioned and stuck on green. Five feet from Dandrie Gun turned his head to tell them once more, Go now, and that's when he sensed movement in his peripheral sight. The bubble inside him erupted and he flung his right arm up, and something struck it hard, glanced off and stung his ear. He twisted and saw Dandrie with his balance back already and his fists loose and moving. His left fist had an opal class ring on it. There was a shred of skin on the ring.

"Get in your car and leave, old fella, and there's not a thing between us." Dandrie was up on the balls of his feet, a little sense in his voice now. "You try and touch me, though, and I won't quit until I'm good and finished."

Later that night, gently explaining his reddened ear to Carol, Gun would omit the "old fella" reference. Would omit, too, his own crude joy at knowing the action was about to start, and at learning that his eyes still picked up speeding things, knuckles and the sharp heels of boots, just as they had the fluttering fastballs of Palmer and Cuellar and Catfish Hunter. It was the eyes you needed, first and foremost, but he would leave that part out; the eyes were principal.

And now they picked up something else: the loss of color starting in Dandrie's lower lip as he understood that the old fella wasn't going to quit. Gun looked to the man's loose fists and saw the left one bunch and accelerate. The jab wasn't half so fast when you were looking at it and Gun turned on it and slapped it away. Now the left again, he thought. It came, and again he slapped it with his palm, so hard it cracked the Plexiglas over the gas pump. Dandrie's lips had lost all redness, and he bobbed for time. Gun smelled clean gasoline and a quick curdled heat from the man's body. He took a step forward: *Come on, try again. Big right hand.* And the right tightened as he'd commanded and swept toward him, and he slowed it down with his clear strong eyes and watched his own hands meet and circle the right wrist of Dandrie, close on it and squeeze. He squeezed as if killing a python. He heard screams but his eyes were on those fingers, constricting and straightening, the ring finger with its nail uncut, a long scoop, the others all chewed ragged.

He felt bones rub against each other inside the python
—felt them slipping and popping—and somehow
that brought him back, and he let Dandrie go.

The two girls were gone.

Dandrie leaned against the bed of his neon-green
truck and made noises like a puking seal.

Gun stood weightless, almost forgetting to move.
He understood that he was smiling and for the moment didn't care. Every muscle in his body, every
endorphin in his brain—they were his friends, every
one of them, and right now they were standing up and
shouting hallelujah.

He walked back to the Dodge with a young man's
step and pumped ten bucks of unleaded, then went
inside and paid the attendant, a kid of sixteen who
was attending mostly to a trash-rock station and a
dirty magazine. Gun laid a ten on the counter. The
kid didn't look up.

By the time he settled back behind the wheel of the
Dodge his adrenaline had fled, and with it his sense of
justification. Never mind that the guy had asked for it.
Never mind about the girls—yeah, the T-shirt was
crummy, but they wouldn't have grown up and become porn queens because of it. If he'd just let things
be, the jerk never would've spoken to the kids; this
way they got to see the nasty shirt *and* the violence. *All
right, Pedersen,* he thought. *Your presence is a blessing
to the children.*

He breathed deeply and slid the car into gear. He
saw Dandrie once more in the rearview glass, the guy
wiping his eyes now with the arm Gun hadn't
wrecked. He thought: Well, great. So you've still got
the eyes, and the moves to back them up. So what?

Driving home, he had to hold the Dodge steady
against a spring wind that had gotten pushier than

most. When he stepped at last onto the porch the sun had utterly lost its influence, and his mother met him at the door and told him Gunsten had departed in a hurry and in reticence, not even troubling to get out of his funeral clothes.

## 7

*I* wouldn't be worried except for what he did to Calvin," Madilyn said. "He fumed over it all the way home. I told him he could just apologize. To Neb anyhow, if not to Calvin. Everyone has boundaries."

She wasn't visibly distressed. But with Madilyn it showed in her voice. It sounded the same, only somehow smaller, as if worry could press down on a person's voice box, tighten it like a copper snare.

"How can you do it? Go on being his conscience, the way you do."

"Oh, Gun." Her eyes understood and forgave his lack of compassion. "He has an *enormous* conscience. The biggest I've ever seen. His conscience is like a disease."

"Maybe it'll suggest that he come home and look after his wife."

"Don't be mad at him. Please. I'm fine." Her voice was so small it might have issued from a medicine jar.

"You've always been fine, Mom." He tried to temper his own loudness somewhat, but impatience rose in his throat. "How long do you think his absolution will take this time? How many days?"

"Maybe that's not what this is."

"Maybe not," Gun said, to help her. The house was quiet. He noticed the wind beginning to pepper the windows with some of last year's leaves. There was perhaps an hour's sun left. "I guess you don't understand either, about the keys."

"He'll talk to me about it eventually."

"I don't know how much time he'll have. Cal Summers will have it all over town soon that old man Pedersen's key ring came up with the body. Dad's going to have to explain, and it won't be a private matter."

She didn't answer. Her back was to him, and it was possible, seeing the fall of her hazelnut hair to her slim, steady shoulders, to imagine that she was young. The quiet impressed itself on him again. "Where's Carol?"

"She fell asleep upstairs. She's a beautiful girl."

"Yes." He rubbed his chin. The whiskers there felt like base-path grit. "I better go find Dad, or try to."

"Do you want to wake Carol? Take her along?"

But he shook his head and pushed the screen door open. Behind him his mother said, "He took the Indian, Gun."

He turned. Madilyn was on the porch, still in her navy dress. She'd removed the onyx brooch and her shoes and was slightly hunched in the wind. She waved good luck, and he smiled back.

Gunsten Pedersen owned a monstrous old motorcycle, an Indian, which had always looked to Gun like it had been built by a yardful of serious gorillas over a long weekend in about 1951. It was heavy and low and as black as oil. It had a surly attitude: Conceived in arrogance and birthed with a jungle roar, that was the Indian, and Gun had never seen his father pamper it. He supposed it didn't need any pampering. Each fall Gunsten would prop the brooding rhino in the back of the barn, where it hulked in shadow, smelling like a bad grudge; and each spring the old man would change the oil, then swing on and kick it in the ribs until it howled and charged.

Gun pounded the accelerator of the faint-hearted Dodge and got a mushy response. The pines on both sides of the road glistened green as the sun slanted in, and the air through the vents smelled like soft new needles and the cold end of daylight.

His father had taken the Indian. He had said nothing before he left. Gun suspected this was not what Madilyn wanted it to be, an impromptu spring ride, a spontaneous up-the-road errand to borrow Ray Hedley's wood chisels. He slowed the car, started to pull over, then realized he was nearly to Copper Strike. Gun let his hometown reflex take him where he needed to go.

The first time Gunsten left so abruptly Gun was a boy and thought his dad had gone and drowned himself in Keweenaw Bay. A decade had passed since World War II ended, taking with it Copper Strike's last desperate swipe at prosperity. But in the spring of 1954 the streets were showing hope again. This was Michigan, after all, and Michigan owned Detroit, and Detroit owned the heart of every independent American who judged his own merit by the length of his automobile. A small group of land speculators, led by the rakish O. Boyer, had showed up in Copper Strike to flatter the city council. O. Boyer owned a pencil-line mustache and a brown fedora and a big clean chin with a hole in the middle of it like Kirk Douglas's. He got his picture in the *Miner,* telling the astonished locals they were sitting in God's own backyard; that by making the proper decisions they would soon have a tourism industry that would make folks forget they had ever seen copper. O. Boyer was the one to make it happen, he said so himself, and to prove it he thumped down a stack of bills and bought two hundred acres of land from the city at twice the asking price. Gun still remembered his father reading the paper that night, tossing his head like a horse shaking off flies, saying, "Madilyn, it's not so easy. These men would make bread out of water and air. They aren't telling the truth, girl."

But there it was, right in the paper, and to celebrate his acquisition O. Boyer said he'd chartered a yacht and was taking his partners and the mayor of Copper Strike and several of the town's "leading businessmen" out to cruise Superior for three days. The boat arrived from Sault Sainte Marie on a Friday. They took off Saturday morning with a healthy westerly snapping the sails. By Sunday afternoon the sky was clogged with tall roiling clouds that twisted with purpose, turning the water the color of galvanized steel. That night Gun had crouched outside the door of his upstairs room while his parents sat down in the kitchen drinking hot chicoried coffee. He listened to them talk through the cast-iron grate in the floor. Their words were almost covered by the wind shearing itself off against the hard chine of roof above his head, but he heard his father say, "They're not coming back, Maddie. Probably foundered already, this wind." Madilyn replied, too soft to hear. Then Gunsten said, resignation dulling his voice, "Not honest men. They would sell this town what isn't theirs to sell. It's not to be allowed to happen."

The worst of the storm came late that night, hard enough to wake the ten-year-old Gun and make him feel his way down the cool maple stairs, the wallpaper trembling against his fingers as he crept. In the kitchen he snapped on the light and heated the remnants of coffee on the stove, then stood at the window to drink it. Raindrops clicked against the glass and then pummeled it and finally snapped horizontal against it, the wind at zenith like a crazed man outside in the yard, flinging fistfuls of dimes.

When Gun woke in the morning his father was gone. He questioned his mother about it.

"I don't know," she said.

"Where he went?"

"*Why* he went." She was stirring oatmeal at the stove. Outside it was raining still, but gently, the wind gone off raging toward Keweenaw Bay. "Gun, do you know what it means to atone? I think he's gone off to atone."

"Did he make a mistake?"

She looked at him, forgetting to stir. Her hair then had been long and pulled back in a ponytail, bound in a strip of blue cloth. "No, sweetie. Some other people did."

"And he's atoning for them?"

"I think so."

That was the first time he'd seen fear in his mother's eyes, and it made him afraid, somehow, to be near her; so he'd gotten up and left the house, walked to the shivering paintless barn and inside it. The Indian was gone and he stood in its resting place, wondering how life was going to be without a dad. He wasn't exactly sure what *atone* meant, or how you did it for somebody besides yourself, but he had an idea. He'd been to Sunday school and knew Jesus had atoned for the sinners. He'd died, too, doing it.

So for days Gun put on a man's face, did his best to take care of his mother and their new, fatherless home. On the morning of the third day he woke early to the burping rip of the Indian pulling into the barn, and when he ran downstairs there was Gunsten, arisen, his clothing beyond wash and his frame gone hollow from fasting; but his face seemed miraculously free of regret or responsibility.

"They came home safe," Gunsten told his wife, and there was accomplishment in his voice. "Gale took them way on out, they were under bare poles and no radio, but they're back and safe."

Madilyn seemed to have something to say, but was having trouble saying it.

"Mr. Boyer has decided against doing business in Copper Strike," Gunsten said. "Know what? Mayor Bergson doesn't seem to care. They tell me he was on his hands and knees, kissing the earth."

And Madilyn still was quiet, and Gun took this as a signal that he should not ask his father where he'd been, or whether he'd actually prayed the boat into staying atop the waves.

He parked the Dodge outside the city-county building and entered. The cigarette smoke adhering to the air seemed older than the place itself. There was a front desk but no one sitting at it. A radio was playing hard-luck country from behind a door that said WOMEN.

It was a lonely place, for a police station, but the town's waning population had long ago reduced and changed the whole nature of policing in Copper Strike. The mining boom had attracted enough roughnecks to fill not only a hearty tavern district but a warehouse-sized jail as well. Now most police calls likely came from passers-through who'd stopped to use the bathroom at the Standard and locked their keys in the car, and the force had been allowed to erode. At some point—Gun didn't know when—the city cops and county sheriff's department had sucked in their egos and made the move to this location—a weak, tan, quilted-looking building behind the courthouse. Averting their eyes, they called it the Law Enforcement Center. They shared a secretary and a dispatcher. They pretended they didn't mind.

Henry Littenen was sitting at Neb's desk when Gun entered the office. He was on the phone, nodding, his face somber as a mutt's at the vet.

"Ah-hah," Henry said, looking at Gun obliquely.

Gun raised his brows, pointed at the door. Want me to leave? he mimed. Henry shook no. He told the phone, "I just called out there, though, and he's gone. Nope, she didn't say where. Is it important?" Gun went to a metal swivel chair with upholstery like the bottom of a bum's trousers and sat. The chair moaned aloud, and Henry put a hand to his brow. He paused, then said, "No, sir, it's just Lisa brought me in some doughnuts. Break time. Yes, sir, I'll tell her. Lisa, honey, Neb says to go mind the phones. We can't both be on break, case it gets busy." This last Henry addressed to Gun. He replaced the phone and exhaled, like Job.

"Smile, Henry," Gun said. "I've been embarrassed before, it goes away."

"You here about a problem?"

"Yup."

"'Course you are. Your dad's lit out, hasn't he? Now, let me give you another one."

"What?"

"Another problem. That was Neb on the phone. Second time in ten minutes. He wants to talk to Gunsten, and he's not in a waiting mood." Henry seemed troubled but also more confident, sitting in the boss's chair. He wasn't jumping all over to explain his own words.

Gun said, "Dad saw him at the funeral and told him he'd come in Monday. There's no hurry."

Henry leaned forward until his long-headed shadow darkened the small Chief of Police signboard on the desk before him. "Listen, Gun. We both know Neb, and he's a gentleman for sure. But he's also a pretty fair old cop, and now, though I hate to say it, he's got something we don't know about."

"Enlighten me."

"I can't. Whatever it is, he wants to talk with your old man about it first."

"Hank, use your brain. You've heard the speculation about my dad killing Harry Summers, and you know what it is. It's horsecrap of the rankest degree. So Harry had the cabin keys—so did *you*, once upon a time, as a kid just married. How *is* Jeannie, by the way?"

"We're divorced."

"That's a damn shame. I'm pained to hear it. Now tell me why this idiot hunch of Neb's has suddenly gained so much credence with you."

Henry Littenen's face seemed to crystallize and shrink at that, Gun's words soaking in so visibly that he wished them back. When Henry spoke it was with an even detachment that hadn't been there earlier. "Like I said, he wants to see your dad. Ask him some questions. Probably some pointed ones, because Neb just now used the word *murder* in the same sentence as *Gunsten Pedersen*. That's uncautious behavior, Gun. You know it as well as I do."

"It sounds to me like Calvin's behavior. You sure that was Neb on the phone?"

"Don't joke, Gun. You came in here with a problem: Your pop's missing. I'm telling you, if you don't round him up soon, you're gonna have a lot of help looking. Lot of guys in uniforms combing the trees."

Gun stood. "I need the keys, Henry."

Henry's forehead contracted above rising brows. "For what? They're evidence."

55

"I think maybe Dad's gone out to the lake. I don't have a set of keys. You do."

"Your folks must have another set."

"Dad's got 'em on his key chain. In his pocket."

"So you think I'm gonna give you the only link we've got to—whoever killed Harry. You, of all folks, thinking I'm gonna just hand 'em over."

"You can toss 'em over, if you like, but hurry it up, the light's going." He reached out his hand, palm up. "Hank, if he's out there, I'll bring him right in and you can sic Neb on him, I don't care. If he's not, then I'll hustle these keys straight back. My word on it."

He had to endure the long lousy business of Henry's distrustful eyes while Henry weighed what Gun's word was worth after such long absence, and then he had to wait while Henry unlocked a file drawer and took out the small cardboard box. And as he shut the office door behind him he had to hear Henry's voice, sounding deadened, say: "I didn't recall you being such a bastard before you left this town."

# 8

*I*t was a Peninsula miracle that you could wake up on a promising morning in May and by sundown be certain you'd entered December. The wind had turned full-heel to the north, and low distant cumulus clouds were bunched like dark grapes out over the bay. The sun was hunched on the west edge of earth and burrowing down in disgrace. Gun drove 56 along the Keweenaw bluffs until he saw the gravel track that angled down toward the water, turned onto it, and worked the Dodge slowly down, feeling the loose skid of stones under rubber.

The cabin he'd bought for his parents looked little changed—little used, for that matter, since he'd handed Gunsten the infamous key ring almost thirty years before. It was the last standing structure on the slope before the grade steepened into clean rock bluff, and it perched outward on a shelf of black bedrock like a birdhouse tacked to a leaning pine. Spit a plug of tobacco out the front-room window, Gunsten said, and if the season was right a silver salmon would rise up and swallow it.

The cabin itself had plain wood-shingle siding beginning to lift at the edges, a wind-darkened tin roof, and bumpy windows paned small to face the Superior gales. The big Indian bike was not parked at the door. No heat trembled from the aluminum chimney. Gun decided to save time and went down the switchback trail to the boathouse.

It sat almost directly below the cabin. It was the real prize of the place, invisible from above because the builder had tucked it back into a natural hollow in the bedrock. He'd been a craftsman, whoever he was; had shipped in honest-to-bayou cypress logs, rough-cut them, and anchored the unrottable timbers into gaps in the rock below the water's surface. There was a string of electric bulbs in there, and a single window on the lake side over the door. The walls and wide-swinging double doors were sawn cypress boards. So was the tight ship's-deck floor, which was U-shaped around the old boat's cradle. The ceiling was a simple slant of bedrock; drill straight up for thirty feet, you'd pierce the welcome mat of the cabin.

For a moment, standing on the cantilevered dock that led to the double doors, Gun imagined he smelled wood smoke and thought he'd lucked out. The boathouse, after all, was where Gunsten would be if he were here at the lake. He'd be sitting in the Hackercraft, alternately messing with the big 130 Chrysler and his King James Version, praying for the patience to finish the restoration job he'd been working at for more than twenty years. But when Gun took the key in his hand (the metal stripped of its nickel finish, he noticed now, but the black ring still smooth as anthracite) and worked the lock open, the air that emerged was as quiet and cold as frost. He peered inside anyway, felt for the dangling electric switch, and chucked it on. The bulbs made a yellow hiss in the damp air. The Hackercraft hung neatly in its webbing. Gunsten's hand tools, his blessed Brukkers and sanding blocks and cans of poly, were piled in thoughtless splendor next to the small barrel stove that vented next to the door.

Gun switched off the light and locked up again, his nostrils confused by the now discernable scent of wood smoke. It was familiar somehow. It had a faint taste of cedar to it—a taste you knew, he understood suddenly, if you had grown up near a townful of Finns. Couple of years back Gun had read in a letter from his mother that Gunsten had finally gone ahead and built a sauna out at the lake place. Recalling the letter now, he smiled in relief. The evening shadows closed on each other for night as he walked up the dock, and the wind began buckling eastward, grieving for autumn. Sweat, Gun knew from experience, was good for a lot of things—good for chasing colds, relieving too much thought, good for afflictions of all sorts. By now, he guessed, a few pounds of guilt would be gone from the old man's pores.

He found the sauna another fifty yards north along the shore, a splintery outhouse-sized box set tidily into a clump of mixed birch and jackpine. The Indian leaned against one cedar wall. Gunsten's clothes were folded and piled on its leather seat.

"Dad. Hey." Gun kept his voice moderate, addressing the box. You didn't like to startle an old naked man in a heat-induced torpor.

"Ten minutes," Gunsten replied. His voice came still and sodden, but not surprised.

"I've got some questions, Dad."

"Ten minutes. Else you can strip and come in here."

The suggestion didn't appeal to him, so Gun leaned back on the gas tank of the Indian and thought about

ways to pry the truth from his father. To hear Henry
Littenen tell it, Neb had come across something
damning, something besides the keys, and whatever it
was, it sure twisted up the dials. For the first time Gun
made himself think objectively about his father's
silence and what might be motivating it. So what the
hell *had* been going on with Harry Summers? What
had the kid been up to that a man as straight-line
righteous as Gunsten Soren Pedersen would approve
of, yet not reveal, even years afterward? If it had been
a simple borrow-the-cabin favor, like with Henry and
Jeannie, why wouldn't Gunsten just say so? Gun sat
on the bike with his back to the dry warmth of the
sauna and let these questions into his mind—they
came with Carol Long's voice—but before any answers arrived he heard the slippage of another car
coming down the rock drive and saw white beams
bouncing between the trees.

It was Neb Summers's Pontiac. Littenen must've
called him about Gun's visit, and Gun felt his impatience with Henry escalate into something nastier. He
needed time alone with his father, and he wasn't going
to get it.

He watched the headlights jounce down slowly and
disappear behind the cabin, listened to the motor
cease and the car door whine and slam. After long
moments the halting point of a flashlight appeared,
Neb feeling his way behind it.

"Dad, Neb's here," Gun said to the box.

Silence. Then, "Can't a man perspire in solitude?"

Neb's shaky beam flitted along the path and lit
finally on Gun. His voice was impaired from lack of
breath. "Huh. Gun. Your dad here?"

"Just taking a little steam, Neb. Want to go in the
cabin? You could sit down."

"Nah. I don't need sitting." But Neb's wind

sounded muddy, and his four-cell flashlight seemed too heavy for his hands.

"Come on." Gun nodded the way, and Neb followed him without protest.

He had to unlock the cabin with the evidential key, but Neb seemed not to notice. The old man was twitching hard. Gun snapped on the fluorescent ring over the kitchen table and pulled up two blue-metal porch chairs. Neb sank into one with visible relief, but his eyes offered Gun only a pinched distrust. His coat was open and his police badge showed, looking large and incongruent, pulling down the loose gray cotton of a shirt that had once fit.

"Henry told me you come out here to find your dad," Neb said.

"Well, I found him."

"Glad of it." The discomfort of standing alleviated, Neb now appeared discomfited by Gun's presence. His breath smelled like an uneasy stomach. His hands worked into his coat pockets and corkscrewed around in there. Gun sensed that quiet, not questions, would propel Neb's tongue.

"Taking his goddamned time," Neb said suddenly, twitching his head at the door. "Damn it, boy, he never explained this to you?"

"Gun. Not *boy*."

"All right. I see I'm the bad guy now, chasing after your pop for no good reason. That's how you're lookin' at it."

Gun didn't answer. Neb's eyes were watery and pink at the corners; they looked twenty years older than his age.

"What if I *have* a good reason? You don't want to think about that, 'course you don't. Listen to me. You believe I *want* to arrest one of my oldest friends? Nuts. You get to where I'm at"—Neb thumbed his sunken chest—"and you'd do anything to *keep* a friend. Nobody wants lonely when they're peering down the grave hole."

"You're out here to arrest him?"

Neb sighed. "No, not yet." He checked the door again. "Where in hell is he?"

"Will you relax? He knows you're here, he'll be along," Gun said, praying the next thing they heard wouldn't be the Indian bike rumbling to life and blasting away out of range.

"Look at me. I'll give you a case of nerves. You know Jim Work?"

"No."

"County coroner. It's no busy career out here in the bush, not like it was, but what is anymore? Back then Jim looked at a lot of stiffs, but the Peninsula's gotten pretty slow. So's Jim, I guess."

"Okay."

"When they found my nephew—his remains—nobody was in a holy rush to get them examined. Wasn't like it was a fresh crime. The lower teeth came out for ID, but the rest—they're just, see, they're goddamned *bones* is all they are, and what good are they to anybody?" Neb's voice had gone threadbare, and he stopped a long moment to patch it up. "Gun, his head was bashed in. You ought to see the boy's skull. There's a big old crack, it was all filled with earth—now you could guess, of course, you could say, 'Somebody smashed Harry one all right,' but who knows? How much equipment's driven over that grave in twenty-five years? Some damn contractor coulda cracked that skull when the boy was ten years dead."

"I'm sorry," Gun said, but Neb had apparently traversed the rough spot, and he went on.

"So what we did was to excavate and put the bones into a morgue box, down the basement of the station, and put Jim Work on notice. You understand there wasn't much urgency."

"Henry gave me to understand my dad's keys were urgent."

Neb's chest heaved as if his lungs were about to wave the white flag. "Hell with the keys. We both know Gunsten's always been generous, even to Henry, the ungrateful shit. Only person upset about the keys is my boy Cal, and he's still waking up soggy in the morning after those jungle dreams of his. No, I meant to talk to your dad on Monday and straighten out that key business. But today," Neb said, his fingers snaking hard now in his pockets, "while we all were at the churchyard, Jim Work got out his pen and brush and had a look at the bones."

Apprehension stirred in Gun. He did not want to speak or to listen. He wanted to rise in slow comfort as though alone, stretch some heat into his refrigerated muscles; he wanted to go find Carol Long and kiss her into silence, fly her down to the deep hot Caribbean and marry her. But he saw Neb watching him, eyes pink and swampy, dry tongue visible in his half-open mouth, and as the tongue moved and began to form words there was a scrape outside and the door blew open, and Gunsten came in wearing pants and no shirt.

"You couldn't wait another day?" Gunsten's thick hair hung down his neck like a soaking white pelt, and his chest had the pink-pale mottle of steamed skin just sensing cold.

Neb withered in his chair and failed to speak. Gun read no fear in the man's posture. Only sorrow.

"What is it?" Gunsten said, and now tiny pointed gooseflesh was spreading over his shoulders and arms.

Neb said nothing but pulled one hand from his coat pocket. He held up a Ziploc bag. There was a corroded metal object in it. The head of an ancient hammer.

"Yours?" Neb said.

Gunsten took the bag, squinted, set it down. "Ball-peen head. Brukker. I guess you know it is, Neb."

"Yeah, I know. That's the hell of it. Now I hope you'll tell me why you killed my nephew with it—and how, God help you, it ended up *inside* his skull."

Gun noticed, though he didn't want to, how that sat Gunsten down and made him look his age for once.

# 9

*H*e woke that night to rain on the roof and lightning playing so far distant it was just a pretty flicker on the walls. The bed was warm enough but something in his mind was nightmare-cold, and he pulled the quilts up high, told his heart to slow down. Had he dreamed? He didn't think so. Hadn't had many dreams since those of Amanda's crash quit coming, years ago now. But under the rain and silent lightning he felt the prickle of a dream yet to come, a dream that wanted him and meant to get him.

He kept his eyes open, watching the lightning pop out over the lake. The rain continued, nothing to build an ark over, but a good slow soaker. It continued until the light show faded into false dawn and still he didn't sleep, and so at last the dream had to come play itself to his wakeful mind, which watched the whole thing like it had no choice. There was darkness, and mud, and of course the rain. There were two men arguing, one weapon between them. A stainless gleam. A shove came, and a swing, another swing carrying a life's worth of malice—then the grave being dug, the slap of the muck, the form of the man doing the work. A tall man. In the dream lightning came from a devilish cloud and turned the man's hair to white.

Gun rose from the bed and put on jeans and a sweatshirt, then sat in a wooden chair next to the window and watched the day in. He hadn't had a nightmare in a long time but decided to be asleep for the next one.

*10*

The small black box, like a cigar box but with a delicate japanned finish, was the one thing about Hunter Watson's office that demanded Gun's attention. Hunter was in the adjoining bathroom, taking a leak that sounded like a year's worth and talking loudly through the door to cover the noise. "Actually, Gun, I was expecting you," he said. "Or your dad, but I didn't think it'd be him. Not that he doesn't trust me," Hunter went on, because he still wasn't done in there, "but he's never struck me as the sort who seeks out a lawyer, even if he needs one."

Gun sat in the leather chair opposite Hunter Watson's desk with his fingers twined behind his neck and tried to figure out that box. It lay on the desk, glossy-backed, compact as a turtle, and tormented him with its likeness to a thing he couldn't place. A similar box, that was all his memory would cough up:

67

a box containing autographed baseball cards, held
with care in the lap of a dangerous eel-like man in a
wheelchair. His name had been Jacobson Cleary and
Gun supposed he was still in West Palm, red-eyed and
hungry, shuffling his cards like a stack of dry scalps
and greedy for the next spring training.

"Ah then," Watson said. He came from the bathroom wearing tennis shoes and an aqua robe that
showed a graying rug of chest hair. The hair on his
head was still black and still heavy—so heavy, in fact,
that his neck seemed to have retracted under the
weight, and his jowls now rested upon his shoulders.
"You'll forgive appearances," he told Gun. "My advice is, don't work out of your home. It's hell on your
customers, and"—he looked pointedly at a maple-
finished wall clock that said 7:50 in the morning, a
Sunday morning—"it's not so good for you either."

"I appreciate your seeing me. I don't have a lot of
time."

"No problem. You're supposed to be off getting
married. No, put your eyebrows back on your face.
You think this town is that asleep, it doesn't know
your business?"

"It's my dad's business I'm here for."

"What, he hasn't explained himself to you? My. His
own boy." Watson smiled, and for some reason Gun
didn't despise him for it. The lawyer's voice was
scratchy with humor, some of which was plainly
self-directed. And how many attorneys, small-town or
not, entertained clients on Sunday morning before
they even got dressed?

"He told me he's innocent. I think he was offended
to have to say it out loud." *There* was an understate-
ment; Gun could still see the glitter in the whites of his
father's eyes.

Watson hunched his head still further down into his
shoulders and leaned into a grin, so that Gun thought,

Sweet God, it's Danny DeVito. Watson leered dramatically. "Come on, Gun, tell me some secrets. Your dad and this boy Harry, who I barely remember—was there anything nasty between them? The kid TP your folks' place on Halloween?"

"Okay, be flippant. Pretty soon it'll make me mean."

"Flippant, my dark hairy butt. Am I the first to ask you that question? Listen, and I'll tell you how things look." He opened a drawer and withdrew a light green legal pad and a Bic. "First there were the keys. They were never a worry, not to anyone but old shell-shocked Calvin. They were worth maybe a cup of coffee and a Danish down at Mona's, but folks know your dad, and they know his nature. The keys by themselves wouldn't be called evidence by any but the infirm and the desperate." Watson was writing smooth letters on the pad as he spoke, using graceful movements that didn't fit with his primal appearance. "The trouble, plainly, will arise from what James Work found inside of Harry's head." The Bic quit rolling, and Watson looked up. "You suppose *he* was surprised—'Hey, what's that rattling around in there?' Dice, perhaps."

"It's unhappy to think about."

"The kid ate it, all right. Work said five of the upper teeth were knocked out or broken off, and by that time Harry was either dead or well on his way. There was some temper behind it. Maybe some revenge."

"It's Dad's hammer."

"Well, of course it is, a Brukker, and Gunsten so prideful about his tools. Still, the hammer isn't the problem—it's his *claiming* the thing so quick." Watson's cheekbones tilted up in annoyance. "He did exactly what he oughtn't to have done—took one look at the instrument and said, 'Yup, it's mine.' Now you've got two items surfacing with the bones, and one of 'em's the murder weapon, and they both belong to the same man."

"Did you expect my dad to lie?" Gun couldn't believe Watson would be so obtuse.

"I said nothing like that. But why do people always feel they have to explain? I don't get it. Watch the news sometime. A reporter goes to the businessman who's under investigation for child molestation and asks why he did it—but does the guy tell the reporter to find an exhaust pipe and inhale? Nah. Some chemical in his faulty brain makes him think if he can just *talk* for a while, his problem will go away. So he opens his mouth, and what comes out is, 'Hey, she told me she was eighteen, it wasn't *my* fault.' What, is restraint not a virtue anymore?"

Gun said, "I think that's a lousy comparison."

Watson waved knuckles in the air. "Look. The problem with your dad owning up to the hammer is that now the police have what looks to them like more than a coincidence. If you didn't know it already, there's going to be an investigation, and my guess is the Bureau of Criminal Apprehension will be in on it. Sooner or later."

Gun waited

"Pretend you're Neb Summers. You're the chief of police in this boarded-up town, and your only help is"—the attorney's nostrils expanded for a moment, gosh, they were roomy—"Henry Littenen, a faithful pard, but not the man you'd wake up screaming for if the Nazis stormed your house in the night. Your fine young nephew is the victim, and your fine old friend is the suspect. And you're dying of cancer. You think he's not going to ask for help?"

"Okay, the BCA. What's to investigate, after twenty-five years?"

"Well, they'll try to establish whether Gunsten and Harry were in proximity when Harry died. Whether they had any history. The sort of details," Watson finished, vulturing in like DeVito again, "you may already know."

Gun let his eyes rest away from Watson as he digested this. That Harry and his father had some unspoken agreement, Gun didn't doubt; he'd pressed Gunsten the previous night, late, the two of them standing on the dark porch regarding their cigarettes with determined reserve. And he'd gotten at least part of the story from the old man: Harry Summers *had* asked Gunsten for the use of the cabin, and Gunsten had agreed. "Why did he want it? He was just a kid," Gun had said.

"He was graduating from high school, and he was older than most of his class. Nineteen. I recall he was expecting to be drafted soon." Gunsten's voice was as calm and smooth as pebbles moving in a distant stream. "He wanted to borrow a private place. A good boy."

"What about the hammer, Dad?"

Gunsten's cigarette, a Lucky, had gleamed with the heat of a long pull. Gun waited with his arms going to gooseflesh inside his sweatshirt. "Well," his father said, "he worked for me some that spring. Just a few hours here and there when I needed a hand. Run-and-get-and-hold, that kind of work." The patience leaked suddenly from his voice. "Sometimes he borrowed things. I expect he borrowed that Brukker."

Gun's eyes focused again and came to rest on Watson's desk, on the japanned box again. He related to Watson what his father had said.

"That's good, that's very good. Takes the tool out of your dad's hands. Gunsten's a lucky one, you know—a little fanatical, but he's lived right as he sees it. People want to believe the best of him."

"I hope that's so."

"It is." Watson tapped two fingers on the slate-top

desk. "You want my diagnosis, it's this: If Gunsten's clean—and as far as I'm concerned, he's like wet Ivory soap—then Harry can't possibly be pinned on him. And even if he did brain the kid—I'm conjecturing, keep your hands in your pockets—I'd say his chances were still better than even. A quarter century. In the law that's geologic time."

Gun stood to go. "You know how long it's been since I've retained a lawyer?"

"Don't talk. It's bad medicine. Do I have your address?" The hairy attorney slid a Rolodex card at him, and Gun signed it with his Stony rural delivery. "Ah," Watson said, spinning the Rolo, "see my fat file. I'm a great collector of these."

That set Gun's mind back on the black box for some reason, and he asked, "What do you collect in there? Souls?" He was aware of sounding geeky and didn't know why he'd asked.

"No, sir. Those are in my Rolodex. This sweetheart"—he pushed the box toward Gun—"is empty. I keep it there because it *looks* like it should hold such pretty things."

Gun lifted the lid. It was smooth as a coat of wax. And empty, or almost. Just an old wheat-back penny, and dust light as smoke, and a couple of dead clay-colored moths, their wings splayed and holeshot, as if they'd flown inside a trap and in desperation had mistaken their own embellishments for wool.

# 11

Gun and Carol drove north, silent. To their left and above them were the high treed hills the fishing tourists from Milwaukee and Chicago liked to call mountains. Higher yet, the western sky was a healthy pink fading to gray, and you could almost hear the sun, long out of sight, sizzle into cold Superior.

The drive was Carol's idea, the destination Gun's. *We need to talk,* she'd whispered in Gun's ear after supper, *get out of here for a couple hours*—this just before Gun and his dad retired to the front porch for their evening smoke.

At a sudden break in the corridor of pines Gun braked and turned right into a gravel drive. Fifty yards in was the narrow two-story frame building, roof pitched for heavy Peninsula snowfalls. Wide wooden steps led up to a wooden porch, and the front door still announced COPENHAGEN SOLD HERE. Gun parked in the gravel lot. It was easy to guess which of the dozen or so cars were local and which were not; people here didn't buy foreign and didn't buy new.

The exterior was asphalt siding, dark-gray imitation brick. A new sign had been attached to the porch overhang, large block letters of unpainted wood spelling out SPEED'S ROUND TEN.

"It's a pretty quiet place, or used to be," Gun said. "We can always leave." He popped open the driver's door and stepped out into the smell of June pines, which was countered by the sour grease exhaust from the kitchen. At the foot of the steps Gun felt a shot of juice in his legs, and he bounded up, two at a time, onto the landing. His mind gave him a quick glimpse of himself as a kid, his mom and dad climbing these steps after him, everyone full to bursting with Saturday-night goodwill.

"You're perky all of a sudden," said Carol. He pulled open the door and followed her inside, his eyes attending to the shape of her there in her cut-off jeans and white T-shirt. Then suddenly gravity and age were on him, and he wished for nothing more than a bottle of beer and some talk. Aimless talk.

Inside, things hadn't changed. Bar on the left, booths along the wall to the right, tables down the middle, pool table at the back, everything still painted the same weak shade of green, a television mounted above the bar. A color set now. The place was busy with middle-aged couples quiet over their food and men sitting alone, watching the Twins and Brewers. In the first booth Gun saw a guy he'd gone to school with. Tried to recall his name, couldn't, and had to settle for a plain hello.

The man nodded and looked away. Gun congratulated himself on his popularity and led Carol to one of the last booths, back near the pool table. Carol seemed stiff tonight, pale, not quite herself, and Gun waited for their conversation to begin, wishing it didn't have to.

On the wall above them hung a faded color photograph of President Kennedy, looking young and visionary. Gun nodded at it. "I was here the night he beat Nixon—with my parents and everybody else. Watched the returns on the TV up there, a black-and-white set then. Whenever Kennedy took a state Speed would start handing out free beer. I was just out of school."

"My parents had a party, too," Carol said. "They liked Nixon." She smiled in a way that said to Gun, Let up a little. Then her eyes wandered over the other photos mounted on the green walls. Most were of boxers, posed shots from the waist up, naked torsos, flat noses, fierce dull eyes. In one corner, mounted on a pedestal and sparring with air, was a bronze pugilist about two feet high. "Who owns the place?" Carol asked. "Speed something, you said?"

"Speed Ruona. Still lives upstairs, far as I know. He was a good middleweight for about two weeks in the forties. Got himself ranked, fought somebody with a name, and nearly got killed. That was it. He came home a hero."

"Like you."

"Except I didn't move home. Or marry a local girl and raise my family here. I didn't dump a load in the County Bank or buy a bar. I haven't spent my years oiling everybody's squeaks around here." Gun nodded hello to the man and woman who'd walked in, wide-built people with recognition in their eyes and reserve in their narrow mouths. "Evening, Bob," Gun said. The couple moved on by and settled with great shifting and sighing into the booth behind.

"You rarely sound bitter," Carol said.

Gun nodded. This was true, and he wasn't sure why

tonight was different. "You were saying we've got to talk. . . ."

A waitress arrived in a cloud of sweet perfume. She was young and seemed thrilled about it, her body so light and smooth and rubbery that Gun was instantly aware of how much effort he was putting out just to keep his shoulders square and his jaw from tipping open.

He ordered a beer, Carol tea.

The waitress said, "Bags or instant?" and Carol said, "Bags," and the waitress flashed her teeth, a natural smile, too, then strode off, barely touching the floor with her running shoes.

"My Lord," said Carol. "She's not even Michael's age." Michael was Carol's grown son. He preferred California. "We're too old for this, don't you think?"

Gun sent her words on a little tour of his brain, then opened the menu to Desserts. He remembered one night eating boysenberry pie in this very booth with his parents. It was the night he'd signed with the Tigers, an eighteen-year-old bonus baby who'd never been off the Upper Peninsula except for trips on Superior in an uncle's boat.

"I don't really mean that, Gun. About being too old. It's just . . . I don't know, there are certain times . . . "

"At our age, more and more of them."

Carol leaned toward him, her eyes focusing hard. "I want it to be right, Gun. I want to feel, when it happens, like it's really happening. Does that make sense? Like you're all mine, and there's nothing at all in your world but me." She reached forward and tapped Gun's forehead, then took his hand and squeezed it. "Like I'm everything, the first nudge and the limit, and no part of you can get beyond me. But I want to be relaxed, too. Comfortable. Which means I've got to have time to get ready, and I haven't had that yet. I just haven't. And listen, if we don't get back tomorrow, like we planned, then I don't think I can see my way clear to pull this thing off." She took a long, slow breath. Her eyes, snapping and green, didn't leave Gun's, and he felt it necessary to engage them with a matching intensity. "Am I clear?" Carol asked.

"You're clear," Gun said. He leaned back as the waitress set a bottle of beer and an empty glass in front of him, a cup of tea in front of Carol.

Gun tried the beer. It was bitter. Carol sampled her tea and added sugar. She said, "So I'm clear. What does that mean? To you?"

"Means I understand what you said, and it makes sense to me."

Carol took another sip from her cup, squeezing her eyes closed. *"Eesh,* this stuff. Am I being a snob, or what? This tea's horrid."

"Yup," said Gun.

"Yup what? I'm a snob or the tea's horrid?"

"I haven't tried the tea."

Carol started to answer but instead closed her lips with forced pleasantness. Then the front door swung open, and Gun, who sat facing it, was staring at the bland face of Calvin Summers, who was staring back. Calvin still had on the cowboy boots that looked too small to be holding feet large enough to carry the rest of Calvin. He still wore the brown polyester dress pants and western-cut polyester suit jacket over a pink shirt. His wide chest tested the strength of the shirt's pearl snap-buttons, and his large, hairy wrists stuck too far out of his sleeves. Though not more than six feet tall in high school, Calvin had been the strongest linebacker in the Keweenaw conference. He hadn't been getting any smaller in the last thirty years.

Gun nodded at him, and Calvin blinked, then went for the bar. He hadn't yet ordered a drink when the door squeaked open again. Calvin turned to look. So did Gun. It was the driver of the neon-green pickup, Gun's pal Dandrie, who walked straight over to Calvin, took the stool next door, and started a one-sided conversation aimed at the side of Calvin's face. This lasted for a minute or two, Calvin looking straight ahead, then Dandrie rose and left the building.

"Wonder what that was all about," said Carol. "The guy looked pretty rough."

Gun shrugged. He didn't tell Carol it was the same guy he'd tangled with at the Conoco station the other night—it didn't seem necessary right now. He could see it *was* necessary, though, to learn something more about Dandrie.

Over at the bar Calvin lifted a shot glass and took it down fast. His shoulders and neck were hunched forward in concentration. The bartender poured again—cognac, it looked like—and Calvin took it down. This happened two more times, and now Calvin's posture was beautiful, boot-camp perfect. He laughed and rocked the bartender backward with an open-handed shot to the shoulder, turned and surveyed the room, his arms spread wide, hands resting easy on the bar behind him. He seemed to be taking in the whole room at once, happily, the way a man admires a sunset.

Carol said quietly, "Let's go."

"I haven't finished my beer. And I'm thinking pie."

"You can be an idiot sometimes."

"I can," Gun agreed.

Across the room Calvin was dropping coins in the jukebox and punching buttons, moving his head to the music before the music had a chance to join in.

"Now we get to learn his taste in songs," Gun said. "My guess, new country."

78

Gun was right. The Kentucky Headhunters, yowling out their brand of longhair hillbilly rock. Calvin stood for a moment, boots planted, his body from the waist up floating and bobbing, then suddenly he was pushing tables and chairs away, clearing a space on the wooden floor. The drinkers and television watchers at the bar had swiveled around to watch. Calvin clapped his hands and strode back to the bar and threw an arm over the shoulders of a young man whose pressed khakis and oversized cotton sweater branded him a tourist. Gun saw the young man stiffen, then nod his head and turn to face his girlfriend; she lifted her fingers to the open collar of her blouse and had time for one step backward before Calvin locked her waist and her left hand in a dance grip. He whirled her off.

"Oh, my God," said Carol.

The young tourist, bereft of his female companion, stood at the bar in a reduced state, grinning weakly. Calvin spun the girl around and around, holding her tight and smiling at the world from over her shoulder.

Back at the bar you could tell the locals by the way they shook their heads, laughed, or spoke into one another's ears. One guy—big, bald, and dressed in camo—called out, "Calvin, hey, that's enough," got no response, and returned dutifully to his beer.

A tourist couple climbed off their stools, leaving pickled eggs uneaten and beer glasses half full. They moved furtively toward the cash register and were paying their tab when Calvin threw his partner in the air, caught her coming down, set her smack on the bar next to her anxious friend, then bolted for the door and caught the fleeing couple on the threshold. He patted the man's arm and bowed to the girl. The man didn't resist, and the woman couldn't—she was half his size.

Carol said, "Poor thing."

"If somebody told him no loud enough, he'd probably go away," said Gun.

The Headhunters were done with their tune, but Calvin with his flying blonde didn't seem to require music. They were still spinning. Gun remembered in seventh grade learning to dance with Miss Herman, the strong, tall gym teacher whose choice for demonstration partner had been, out of necessity, the biggest boy in class: Gun. He felt sharp sympathy for Calvin's reluctant partner and recognized the look on her face that said, "I'm lost, save me."

Gun considered doing just that. But the tune that kicked in next was thankfully downbeat, a melancholy ballad, Wynnona Judd without her lovely mother and doing just fine. Calvin put on the brakes and moved into a love grip. Plastered himself against the girl, maneuvered her over to her man, and released her.

The man said, "Thank you," stupidly.

Calvin raised his arms and spoke to the room. "Ladies," he said, "I'm yours." He turned back to the bar and snapped his fingers at the bartender, who shook his head and looked away. "Damn it, Stanley, a guy works up a thirst. Move your butt!" The bartender leaned close and spoke into Calvin's ear. Gun watched Calvin rise up on his stool and look quickly to his right.

In the doorway to the kitchen stood an old man wearing a tight-fitting turtleneck sweater, army green. He had a muscled chest, and his stomach looked like something he worked hard on. His white hair was cropped close, and his large nose wandered considerably from roots to bulbous tip.

"That's Speed," Gun said to Carol. "He could always smell stuff like this."

"Living upstairs, he'd be deaf not to have heard."

"He *is* deaf. Has been since his last fight."

Speed smiled at Calvin, his blue eyes as warm and bold as glazed pottery. "Give him what he wants, but just one," Speed instructed Stanley. "Coffee, too, on the house."

Calvin nodded now, agreeable. He swallowed the next cognac and reached a finger to his back pocket for his wallet. He left a few rumpled bills on the bar next to his untouched cup of coffee and made straight for Gun and Carol.

From behind the bar Speed called out, "Watch yourself, Cal, buddy. Hi there, Pedersen."

In response Calvin, without turning, hoisted an arm and wiggled his fingers in the air. He stopped at Gun's table and folded his arms across his chest.

"Don't tell me I'm next," said Gun. "I don't move so well anymore."

"Thought about asking your lovely friend here, but figured you might not like it so much." Calvin hadn't recovered the smile he'd lost when the slow music began. His white face was vegetable bland. He was drunk.

"Ah, I doubt if *she'd* have liked it so much," Gun said.

Calvin shrugged, and Carol said, "I *am* tired. No offense, Calvin."

"None taken." Calvin sighed and shifted weight from one leg to the other. He said, "Gun, let's step outside."

"Huh?"

"That didn't come out right." He squeezed the bridge of his nose and shook his head. "We've got a few things to discuss. Straighten out some shit. Five minutes."

"Sit down, join us."

"I'd rather just you and me . . ." Calvin blinked and looked hopefully toward the door.

Gun looked at Carol. Her green eyes were resigned, not angry. With a small move of her head she told him to get.

He said, "The boysenberry," then he got up and led Calvin to the door and outside.

Stars had returned to the skies of Upper Michigan, Gun noticed. The Big Dipper was emptying whatever it held into Lake Superior, and the half moon burned so brightly you could make out the colors of the automobiles sitting in the parking lot.

"Sometimes . . . up here," said Calvin, his face turned to the sky, "you almost forget they're out there."

Gun was silent.

"Drive a man crazy," said Calvin, "unless something else does first."

"There's always something else, isn't there?"

Calvin agreed. He clunked down the wooden stairs off the short front porch of Speed Ruona's bar. Gun followed, not sure if the man's need was to speak or be spoken to.

"What a day," Gun said.

Calvin nodded. "Harry used to say, 'Let's just for*get* this sucker.' It was something he could do, too. Just put it all out of his head, go out and have a good old time anyway. Like after a bad game or something."

"You played a little, too, right? Outfield?"

"Second fiddle," said Calvin.

"And football. All-state linebacker, as I recall."

"In our family it was baseball that counted." Calvin turned and looked at Gun. The moon caught in his eyes, which had the lazy-dog focus of a boozer. His voice, though, had a good sharp edge on it. "We were seven years old, Harry and me, and Fourth of July down on the bay, that festival they had every year. All

82

those games and shit for kids. And prizes. They probably still do it, I don't know. But Harry and me thought we'd enter this one contest, the stone throw. First prize was a Wilson glove, Mickey Mantle, worth about twenty bucks even then. Beautiful leather, sort of bronzy. They had it sitting there with the other prizes in the back of a pickup truck for the kids to slobber on. Harry and I had ourselves needing it in the worst way."

Calvin bent down and picked up a quarter-sized stone from the gravel lot. He stayed on his haunches and tossed the stone from hand to hand, dropped it, picked it up again. He straightened upright, groaning. "See that car there?" he asked, pointing. It was an American make, a Chevy about ten years old, parked next to a brand new Toyota. Both cars were facing the other way. "My vehicle, so don't worry," Calvin said, and he wound up, brought his arm back, and threw the stone in a sidearm whip, with force. Gun heard the sharp crack of glass and saw the left rear taillight of the Toyota go dark.

"Shit," said Calvin. He shook his head, disappointed. "I'm better than that. Somebody's gonna be pissed." He walked over to the car, and Gun went along. "Don't say anything, all right? When you go back in? I don't need this right now."

Gun said, "What about that throwing contest down on the bay?"

"Didn't fare any better then. And that's when I was sober." Calvin laughed.

"Harry beat you."

Calvin dug into his eye sockets with a thumb and forefinger. "Harry was my cousin, Gun, and there wasn't much about him that wasn't near-to-God perfect. I loved the hell out of him for it, too. That's the

truth. And hated always coming in on his ass-side.
This English teacher ran the contest that day and
made us go in alphabetical order. There was about
eight or nine of us gonna throw, and Summers was the
last name up, and Calvin comes before Harry. So it
comes down to me and him. After I threw I figured I
had it won. I beat those other kids by fifty feet at least,
and up in my mind I'm already making catches with
that Mickey Mantle. Then Harry comes up, and it's
like watching the Olympics on TV the way he moves,
legs and arms all going around like a wheel, and the
stone—I was watching it go, and it plain wouldn't
come down. He made it look like nothing, like if you
couldn't throw the way he could you must be a retard
or a girl. He got the glove, and that was how it went
from then on, him and me. It wasn't easy, but for
me there wasn't anybody else like him. Nobody. You
gotta see that. Then all those years . . . and then his
bones, and your dad's key ring turning up like that?
And the hammer? Shit, even *you've* gotta see how it
looks."

Calvin slumped against the rear end of his Chevy.
"There's no apologizing for what happened this afternoon with your dad. Just happened. You'd've done
the same thing in my place. Anybody would."

Gun said nothing as Calvin peered at him, waiting
loose-eyed for agreement or something else Gun
couldn't give him.

*"Wouldn't* you?" asked Calvin. Gun heard a long,
low, miserable fart escape the man.

"You better get some sleep," Gun told him.

Calvin seemed for a few moments to brighten, to
acquire a new, harder shape. He looked ready to
smash something. Then at once the tightness went out
of him. "You would've," he said, drawing the keys to
his Chevy from the pocket of his trousers.

# SACRIFICE

"Good night, Calvin." Gun turned and walked back toward the bar. Mounting the steps, he heard a sharp thud. He turned around. Under the full moon Calvin drew back his foot like a television cop and kicked the front door of the old Chevy, then kicked it again and again, grunting from the effort.

# 12

The clear sky had remained so into daylight, and Gun drove through downtown Copper Strike impressed by what a strong morning sun could accomplish on the face of a town well advanced toward ruin. Main Street was half a dozen bankruptcies from dead, and the harsh light showed every missing brick, every lost pane and boarded-up door of the red-brick storefronts. The sun lit the carved cornices of the century-old buildings: Lupin 1889, Kokkenen 1890, Anderson 1901, the bank, the dry goods, the hotel. There was the empty post office—a new one stood at the edge of town—and across from it the Carnegie Library, lost to fire years ago and still black at the windows. Gun drove slowly and took note of the weak vital signs. A barbershop in what once had been a shoe store. A craft shop in the old hardware. A chiropractor in the movie house. (Gun imagined patients with crooked backs lined up inside, eating popcorn.) A video store in a former bar.

In part, Main Street's decay was connected to the new mall east of town. But the real problem was older and much deeper. The Peninsula with its store of copper underground was no longer worth mining. At its peak in the teens and twenties Copper Strike had been a city of twenty-five or thirty thousand. Now only six or seven thousand were still here, and most depended more or less in equal parts on Michigan's welfare system and the U.P.'s tourist trade. The last mine had been closed for twenty-five years.

Gun turned left at the old fire hall, gutted and crumbling, and headed for the high school. Last night, after watching Calvin punish himself on the Chevy, Gun had gone back into the bar and over boysenberry pie asked Carol for one more day. Hunter Watson no doubt had it right. Gunsten was safe for the time being. Plenty of legal elbow room. Still, Gun's father had put seventy-five years of himself in this scratch-for-a-living country, and the single thing he had to show for it was a reputation for honesty in work and talk. It was something to protect.

All Gun wanted for now was time enough to ask the questions that begged to be asked. One more day, he told Carol, and then his conscience would allow him to go off and get married, forget about everything for a couple weeks. Come back here later.

Carol had relented—against her better judgment, she pointed out.

Gun steered the Dodge into the parking lot of the school. This morning the playground was free of kids, but just east of the building in a square of bright sun next to the merry-go-round two young men were spray-painting a line of desks dog-turd brown.

One man wore a ponytail, and the other's head was shaved to a line two inches above the ears. As they worked they watched a small television attached to a heavy-duty orange extension cord running through a window into the school. Gun walked up to them.

"Don't mean to disturb your work," he said. "I'm wondering where I might find Mr. Tokannah." He wondered to himself if he'd ever called the man mister before, doubted it.

The man with the shaved sides just stared, nothing in his face suggesting comprehension, let alone intelligence. The ponytail guy said, "You mean Green?"

"Yeah, where's he at?"

"Around back, I think. Somewhere in the dirt."

Gun said thanks and left the workers to their morning television. He walked across the grade school softball field, down past the tennis courts, and around the back of the high school building to the athletic fields—except they weren't there any longer. In Gun's day the baseball and football fields had been joined like Siamese twins, left and center forming the lion's share of the gridiron. Now everything was gone—no infield, no wire-mesh backstop, no goalposts, no wooden bleachers, no grass. In their place was a deep rectangular hole large enough to play a ballgame in and, surrounding it, hills of black dirt streaked with reddish clay. Caterpillars, trucks, and assorted earth-moving machines were scattered about, quiet, nobody on the job today.

Gun whistled his surprise. He had known what he was going to see but was still unprepared. Here was a place, after all, that still figured in his dreams at night, and to see the land dug up and laid open was

an assault on his memory. It felt lousy. He stood
next to the corner of the old high school, rested a hand
on the cool brick, and waited. Closed his eyes and
brought it all back the way it had been: the skinned
infield and wooden dugouts, the lopsided outfield,
deep to right and center, short to left. He imagined
himself at the plate, saw his body respond to a fast-
ball, turn on it and drive the ball deep and high,
over the left field snow fence, over the cars parked
behind it, over the white concrete bus barn that
stood to the west of the playing field. He remembered the feel of his legs pumping, the sensation
of his father's eyes on him as he touched each base
with his steel spikes. He remembered the sound
and pleasure of stomping the hard rubber of home
plate.

Gun took a breath, sniffed the dirt and ruin. He
opened his eyes. At least the press box was still here,
standing above the western edge of the field. It was a
small square building on twenty-foot stilts, and Gun
saw that somebody was up inside it now. A face
appeared and disappeared in the wide front opening:
Green Tokannah.

Gun tried to recall if he'd ever really spoken
with the man. Tokannah had been school janitor since
Gun could remember. The kids—and everyone
else in town, for that matter—had always called him
Green, whether because of his green work clothes
or because it was the name his parents had given him,
Gun didn't know. He was short and round with a
bulbous nose and full, veiny cheeks, a voice low and
guttural.

Gun remembered the time in fourth grade when
Green had scared him so badly that Gun had peed his
pants. It was a late winter afternoon, history class, and
the pull-down map of the Spanish exploration routes

would not retreat into its cylinder. Miss Hansen thought Green might be able to fix it and sent Gun to find him. She suggested he try the boiler room, a place Gun knew about but had no desire to visit. Exercising what small courage he had, Gun descended to the lower floor, walked to the very end of the dark concrete hall, and knocked on the heavy steel door. No one answered, so Gun pushed it open and peeked inside. A single large bulb lit the cavernous space, and the boiler itself—huge, round, and filthy green in color—sprouted pipes like massive tentacles. Off to one side was a desk, and beside it a large metal file cabinet. Above, on the cement wall, was a pegboard decked out with neatly arranged tools. Gun felt the cold buzzing thrill of trespass in the lining of his stomach.

He'd taken a couple of steps toward the desk when a short bark sounded from the corner. Gun's neck muscles choked him, and his bladder let loose. He saw Green lean forward from behind the file cabinet, then heard the man bark again. But this time Gun could make out words. "Whadya want?"

Gun ran, the front of his pants already sticking cold against his skin.

The press box stilts looked like plain old telephone poles, and bolted to one was a steel ladder. Gun stepped onto the first rung and said, "Anybody home?" He heard the same old bark and saw Green's face lean out over the opening in the floor.

Gun mounted the ladder and climbed into the press box. Green looked older, but not by much. He still wore the same style of trousers and shirt, same drab green color. His face was redder now, but not as full—some of the weight had fallen into jowl. He looked at Gun hard for a moment, as though figuring, then recognition showed in his pale, mucky eyes. He looked away.

"Gun Pedersen," said Gun, and he put out his hand. Green Tokannah's was small, hard, and meaty, and his handshake was fast. Then the janitor bent down quickly and started yanking at some electrical wires at the front of the press box.

"Tearing out the PA?" Gun asked.

Tokannah braced his left knee against the wall, and he pulled hard. A foot and a half of black-coated wire snaked free of the conduit. Green tossed it aside and coughed into a fist.

"You got a minute to visit?" Gun asked.

Green stood and leaned out the front window of the press box. With a large screwdriver he went to work on one of the old-fashioned speaker horns. Gun tried to recall whether Green was deaf in addition to being antisocial and a drunk.

"I'd like to hear anything you might know about Harry Summers," Gun said. Green's head rotated a notch in Gun's direction. He blinked his milky eyes. "You must have been close by when they found him."

"Armp," Green said, and Gun remembered this: The janitor used these extra syllables, expulsions of raw voice and air that made his torso bob. Other people just cleared their throats.

Green swung back in and tossed a lag bolt on the floor. "Whole thing's going down," he said. "Tomorrow."

"The press box."

Tokannah nodded. "Helped put it up in forty-six, this box." He laid down his screwdriver and looked out over the piles of earth. "Filthy mess."

"That's a few years ago. You were a young man," Gun said, though it was next to impossible to imagine him without the broken vessels in his nose or the large belly. What Green was, it seemed, he had always been: a man of absolutely no account, hopelessly short of respectability, yet too predictable to interest the scandalmongers. Apparently he did his job well enough to keep it, even if he did drink every cent he made at the Sidewalks Tavern on the south side of town.

"Want to show me the spot?" Gun asked him.

"Wouldn't hurt none, I guess," and Green nodded for Gun to climb down first.

Tokannah moved quick and surefooted through the loose dirt, making his way around the western and southern edges of the building site. He kept his eyes on the ground. "Never woulda found him at all if it wasn't for me," he said.

"Yeah?"

"They was using the backhoe, cleaning up the edges of the cut, getting ready for the block to go up. Right along over here, see? That's when I told 'em they better shovel that thing outa there." Green pointed at the upended dugout not far from the edge of the main hole. "Wouldn't look right, baseball dugout parked twenty feet back of the new school like that. And I told 'em so. Shit-for-brains they got for a foreman. And this boy on the backhoe gives me a look, then wanders off to find the boss. Which agreed with me."

"So you were here when they hit the bones?"

"He was digging the concrete footings with a Bobcat, and I saw 'em down there when the scoop swept through like a pile of big sticks, black almost." Green Tokannah moved over to the wooden dugout, which was perched on its slanted roof. He rocked it with one arm. "Wasn't much to look at."

"My mother wouldn't agree with you," Gun said.

It was clear to see where the bones had lain. A few feet behind the footings of the dugout was an area that had been trampled flat. It was only a yard or so deep, and as wide and long as a grave. It *is* a grave, Gun thought. This is where Harry's been hiding out all this time.

"Surprised there's no police tape roping it off," said Gun.

"It come down yesterday, after the funeral. Henry took it. Nothing to save here anymore." Tokannah grunted. "Everybody and their dog's been through this dirt."

"Let's go," Gun said.

"You don't wanta get in there and look around some?" Green nodded at the grave. He looked surprised.

"I just wanted to see it. Now I saw it." Gun took a couple of steps away, then stopped and turned. "I also wanted to ask you something," he said. "It's been on my mind ever since I heard where they found him, and I suppose it's been on Neb's mind, too. And Henry's. Maybe they already asked you."

Green Tokannah—standing next to the overturned dugout, one hand resting on a corner of it, large round stomach jutting over his belt—looked like a man with much on his mind. His dish-soap eyes were off in the hills. He shook his head.

"I'm wondering," Gun said, "how it was that Harry got put in the ground here, in this spot, and you never knew about it. You're the guy that kept this field in shape. You worked this grass and dirt every day. It just doesn't make sense. How does somebody dig a grave here and keep that grave a secret? Of course Neb must've already asked you that."

The old janitor cleared his throat and spit. He nodded his head. "Yeah," he said softly.

"And what did you tell him?"

Green didn't open his mouth, just rubbed his eyes with his fingers.

"Well?" Gun asked.

"Same thing I'll tell you. Wish I could say."

"Meaning you can't, or you won't?"

Green shook his head. "Help me God, I don't know how this ever came to be."

# 13

From the way Calvin had been acting, and Neb, too, both grabbing onto grief with all their howling, familial strength, you would've thought poor Harry's memory had no other shattered hearts to call home. This wasn't the case.

Harry's mom and dad lived in a plain white bungalow on the low side of the town, next to the smelting plant ruins. At the funeral and burial Gun hadn't spoken with them. Few people had. They'd looked unapproachable, dressed as they were in unseasonable black wool, their faces moist and white, their limbs moving in a kind of wobbly slow-motion.

Lifetime Copper Strikers, they operated the florist shop, Mavis arranging flowers, Myron delivering. They looked alike, the two of them, tall and lean with classically well-put-together faces. They were athletes, bowling and golfing together in the mixed leagues. Individually they'd won trophies in statewide competitions. All this, and Myron was a Korean war hero, too, a decorated POW who'd survived the winter of '50–'51 in the camp called Death Valley. Yet they were the kind of people you didn't think about unless you were standing on the street corner with them, talking. They went about their lives with a minimum of noise and parade. Harry, their only child, had been the only reason Gun knew them as more than acquaintances.

The winter after Gun's first season with the Tigers they'd invited him for dinner a few times to pick his brain on the matter of son Harry's baseball future. And though Gun hadn't been much help to Harry's career—the boy had disappeared the summer after graduating—he'd enjoyed getting to know the family.

The car clock showed eleven A.M. as Gun pulled to a stop in the Summers driveway. The house appeared to be shut tight, and the dog kennel beside the garage was empty. Gun went to the door anyway.

Myron answered the first knock. He wore creased blue jeans and leather slippers. His face held few lines. His eyes weren't red.

"Hello, Myron." Gun looked for evidence of being unwelcome. There was no telling what kind of talk was going around about Gunsten.

"Gun?" Myron frowned for an instant, face crumpling. Then he composed himself, shook his head, and took hold of Gun's shoulder. "Come in."

The house was dark but for the kitchen down the hall, where a fluorescent ring bulb burned away. "I didn't think I'd find anybody home. No dog in the kennel," Gun said.

"No dog, that's right," said Myron. "How about coffee? Just made it." He led Gun into the kitchen and seated him at a small oak table. He poured coffee and sat down himself.

There had always been a clean-shaven, military, almost boyish neatness about Myron Summers, but now he looked like what he was, a guy not even close to young anymore whose kid had turned up dead. His eyes carried a gray depth, and he hadn't shaved for days. The stubble on his chin and cheeks was salt-and-pepper.

As he lifted his cup to drink he spilled coffee on his lap. He spilled again as he sipped. Coffee ran down his chin, and he dabbed himself with the cuff of his shirt.

"I liked Harry a lot," said Gun.

"He was a hard kid not to like, wasn't he?"

"I liked him as a ballplayer, too." Gun was thinking of the couple times he'd gone out to the park with Harry and hit balls at him.

Myron looked off, shaking his head as if he didn't want to hear any more. "All those years it felt like everybody in town forgot we even had a son. No one ever saying anything . . . like it was something to be ashamed of." Myron closed his eyes and spread his fingers out on the edge of the table. "His mother and me—do you suppose we could ever forget, for even a day? Do you think Harry was out of our minds for more than an hour at a time? And now he comes back dead, and suddenly *everybody* remembers. Everybody bawling and grabbing us. It's hard to appreciate." Myron opened his eyes.

Gun kept his silence.

"I understand what you're doing here, Gun, and I want you to know I don't harbor any bad feelings toward your dad. Neb keeps me up to date, like he ought to"—Myron shook his head—"but I've got to say the stuff they turned up so far doesn't mean much to me. It's all too easy. I've known Gunsten all my life. . . ."

From down the hall a female voice came drifting into the kitchen, airy and high. "Honey, I smell coffee." Myron stood quickly and went to the cupboard. He grabbed half a dozen bottles of prescription pills and started opening them one by one and shaking out a pill or two from each.

The voice came again, a bright, high birdsong. "Honey, my meds. I'll take them with my coffee."

Gun watched Myron scoop the pills from the countertop into one hand, then pour coffee. "Be right back," he said, and his eyes met Gun's in an appeal for understanding.

Minutes later, entering the kitchen, Myron said, "It's not as bad as it might look, Gun. Most days she's fine. Gets up, makes ham and eggs. She'll get better." There was nothing like conviction in Myron's tone.

Gun waited.

Myron sipped coffee, his eyes wandering to the window above the sink. Outside the view was long and green, and the distance seemed to provide a comfort to him. "She likes to keep things in their place, neat and orderly. She likes to know what to expect, plan ahead. Me, too, for that matter. It's a good way to be, as long as life more or less cooperates. When it doesn't you end up beating the hell out of yourself."

"You seem to be getting through it," Gun said.

"Today's one day," said Myron. "You know?"

Gun pointed with his empty cup toward the coffee maker. "Do you mind?" Myron shook his head, and Gun went to the counter. "I was wondering what you thought when he first disappeared. I mean, was Harry just gone one day?"

"That's about it. And he kept being gone."

"Did part of you think he might have planned it? At the time folks talked about Canada. Did that seem like a possibility?"

"Absolutely not. Harry wouldn't have run like that." Myron scowled. "Lots of talk went around—all bullshit, if you knew Harry. First off, he wasn't scared. Second, leaving the country would've been leaving baseball. Two good reasons. No, I never gave it a thought."

Mavis appeared in the hall just off the kitchen. She wore a light green flannel nightgown that came to her ankles. In the hallway shadow she seemed fit and young, unchanged. A large green handkerchief was tied tightly about her skull.

"You look wonderful—hello," Gun said.

"Thank you." She entered the kitchen slowly, the fluorescent light adding years to her. Wrinkles appeared around her eyes, a slackness of flesh in her throat and along the jawline. She said. "We always kept a dog, Gun, ever since Harry left. Myron himself built that kennel for Harry's dog."

"I think I remember," Gun said. "Harry had that yellow lab for hunting."

"And we've had a couple dogs since. I like dogs." Mavis turned to Myron, and Gun saw her eyes change. "I like dogs," she repeated.

"Leave it alone," Myron told her.

Mavis coughed into one hand, an unfeminine blast. She walked to the sink and looked out the window, peering east toward the garage and kennel. Her fingers played with the knot in the handkerchief, which had come loose at the back of her neck. She freed the two ends of the cloth and twisted them with her fingers. As she pulled it back tight around her head Gun got a glimpse of her skull, hairless and pink. "I'd like another dog," she said, turning back into the room.

Myron closed his eyes.

"Do you know why our dog is gone?" she asked Gun. The disturbance in her eyes told him he didn't want to. He shook his head and saw Myron plant his hands on his knees in preparation for rising from his chair.

"Because," Mavis said, "last week, the morning after we found out about Harry under the ballfield, Myron went out to the kennel with his shotgun." Her face was set up hard as concrete, chin high, eyes barreling into Myron. "That poor dog knew it, too, the way he was crying."

Myron stood. "I think Gun's gotta be going," he said.

"Gun," Mavis said, "there's an uncle of Harry's that lives in Toronto. A great uncle."

Myron said, "Mavis." His voice was tired.

"He and Harry were close," she went on, her eyes brilliant and fastened to Gun. "He's over ninety, lives in Toronto. You should talk to him."

"Mavis isn't feeling well," said Myron. He sighed and turned toward the door, motioning to Gun with his head.

"His name is Maxwell Summers," said Mavis. "He lives on Queen Street."

Myron walked slowly, head down, toward the front door. Gun followed him.

# 14

Gun drove down Main Street to verify that all the old cafés were indeed closed up: Bernie's, The Blue Parrot, Auntie Mo's. Then he headed out to the mall on the edge of town. He parked the Dodge, went inside the white air-conditioned plaza, and walked the wide white corridors past several clusters of molded plastic waiting benches. To his right and left were stores with names and appointments identical to stores in similar malls throughout the country. People now seemed to require predictability above all else, sameness. And shopping had become the national sport. It made a guy embarrassed for his times.

Next to a jewelry store full of mirrors and hair-sprayed clerks Gun found a restaurant called The Copper Mine with old black-and-white photos of miners displayed above the yellow plastic booths. The pasties were all right, though a little short on meat,

101

and the coffee was, as Steve Cannon would say back home on WCCO, not adequate.

Gun picked up the sports section of the Houghton paper and learned that his two favorite teams were struggling. The Twins were hunting a .500 record, still fighting off their winter sleep. Detroit was eighteen and thirty, way down there next to the Indians. Gun winced and tossed the sports aside. What he saw on the lead page of the variety section made him lean in for a closer look. He felt his stomach warm and tighten.

"Diane," he said aloud, and a waitress flowing past with a coffeepot applied the brakes and set a fist on one hip.

She said, "Diane's the other one, Jake. Something *I* can do for ya?"

Gun waved her off and held the paper up to better light. The photo was overly posed but flattering all the same. The format was vertical, two columns wide by about six inches high. Diane Apple stood in front of a batting cage, smiling, legs crossed at the ankles, her slender figure leaning casually against a baseball bat. She wore a Toronto Blue Jays cap. The headline said, "Scriptwriter hits grand slam, filming begins in Toronto."

The piece that followed was full of the typical stuff about sudden money and the long, hard road to success. Nothing at all about the Diane that Gun knew. As he read the article he remembered the letter she'd sent him in the fall. In it she'd mentioned this film deal, the spring shooting schedule. More to the point, she had asked him if there was any reason to think there might be a future in what they had started together in Florida the winter before. Gun hadn't responded. Hadn't been in a position to at the time. There had been Carol, of course, but also the commotion surrounding Dick Chandler's boy. Important things to do. Besides, hearing from Diane in that way, on paper, had made her seem like a lovely image from a book or a movie, and his brief episode with her in Florida a scene that had little to do with his life back home on Stony Lake. He put the letter in a desk drawer and tried to forget about it—about her—with more or less success, depending on the day.

Gun thought about the Summers uncle in Toronto. Then he promised himself that any trip to Toronto to visit Uncle Max would be just that, a trip to visit Uncle Max.

Before leaving the mall he found a pay phone and dialed the sheriff's office. Neb was there but probably shouldn't have been. His voice sounded like it was coming from the bottom of a galvanized water bucket.

"I talked to a couple folks today about Harry," Gun said. "I don't want you to think I'm sneaking around behind your back."

"Talk to whoever you like. This is your hometown, Gunsten's your old man." If Neb was angry, it was hard to tell. He was too weak to sound anything but sick and tired. He just waited there on the other end of the line. No questions.

"I talked to Green Tokannah, for one."

"All right."

"I told him it struck me as odd, him not knowing about a grave on his ballfield." Gun let a moment pass. Neb didn't try to fill it. "I'm wondering, Neb. Did you raise this subject with Green?"

Neb huffed a little, from shortness of breath or disgust, Gun couldn't tell. "You *ask* Green if I did?"

"Yeah."

"Checkin' up on me."

"Yeah," said Gun.

"What'd Green tell you?"

"What are you telling me?"

"I'm saying of course I asked him," said Neb.

"That's what Green said."

"I'm glad for the high level of trust here, friend. Shit."

Gun didn't apologize. "Do you believe him?" he asked.

Neb sucked a breath, coughed. "Don't know. I guess I don't disbelieve him."

"I do," Gun said. "I'd say it's near impossible not to disbelieve him. Summertime, he lives on that ballfield. Or did then."

"It was behind the dugout, for God's sake. And who's to say what time of year the body got put there? Seems you're makin' a leap."

"I also spoke with Harry's mom and dad," Gun said.

"Edifying conversation?"

"Mavis mentioned a great uncle of Harry's in Toronto. Said I oughta talk to him. Myron was not happy."

"Mavis isn't right upstairs anymore."

"Maybe. But I think somebody better check the guy out. What's his name? Max?"

"Uncle Max doesn't know shit, I can tell you that right now." Neb started hacking into the phone, and Gun pulled the receiver from his ear, waiting for him to finish.

When it was quiet Gun said, "You think maybe Harry had a mind to dodge the draft?"

"What'd Myron tell you?"

"He told me no."

"I agree. Harry wasn't chickenshit."

"Well," Gun said, "I think I'll go up there anyway and have a talk with your uncle Max while he's still alive to talk to. He's over ninety, says Mavis."

"If you need to go, by all means go," said Neb. He barked air.

"You sound real interested in getting to the bottom of things," said Gun.

Neb sighed. "Friend, let me lay things out here. Yeah, I'd like to know what happened to Harry. The kid was my nephew, my own boy Calvin's best buddy. Let's realize, though—he's been dead a while. He's been dead since Nixon's first term. Harry's been dead longer than he was alive."

Gun waited to see where this was heading.

Neb cleared his throat and found a better voice. "You're wrong, Pedersen, if you think I'm not doing my job. I'm doing what needs doing, and it's goddamn hard. You think I liked having to show that hammer to Gunsten? That ring of keys? But there they were, the only pointers we got so far. Not that they mean much of anything, in and of themselves. And of *course* I talked to Green. But the man's ignorant—generally speaking, yeah, but ignorant about that grave, too. I believe him. He's not smart enough to lie about something as big as bodies in the ground."

"The man isn't stupid," Gun said. "He's a drunk."

"Drink that much for that long and you're stupid. Don't bullshit me, Gun—I live here, I know him, and he's a goddamned idiot."

"You sound about ready to call it quits."

Neb laughed. "This is great. His old man's the only suspect in a murder case, and he wants me to push harder."

"Damn right I do," Gun said. "But as long as you're not going to, I guess I'll have to."

Gun hung up and walked out to his car. The day was turning warm. He got in behind the wheel and sat there for a while thinking.

Across the street at the municipal swimming pool a woman not so much younger than himself stepped out of her car and walk toward the changing house. She was in great shape for her age, a good straight back, a gliding walk, and he bet she could still wear a two-piece suit without embarrassing herself. He thought of Carol Long on a sizzling white beach, the ocean washing in on her toes. He saw Carol, in his mind, turn to give him a look, her bare green eyes stirring things up.

What could he possibly lose, he asked himself, by going off and getting married, then coming back here in a couple of weeks, picking up where he'd left off? Harry, after all, had been underground for twenty-five years.

# 15

Sitting out on the front lawn with Madilyn and Gunsten, Carol looked more like a daughter-in-law than Gun had thought possible, leaning back on the homemade cedar chaise longue, her legs crossed at the knees, hair lifting in a warm gust from the south. She was even smiling. Her face was turned toward Gunsten, who gestured with his hands as he spoke. There was a bucket of ice on the grass with a few bottles of blackberry soda, Gunsten's favorite.

"He's telling me about the mines," Carol said as Gun stepped from the car.

"The old horror stories," Madilyn put in.

"Well, *she* hasn't heard them before," said Gunsten, "and I figure it don't hurt, either, your wife-to-be knowing how close I came to never getting conceived in the first place, since if I don't arrive, then you don't either, Gun, and she doesn't have a man to marry."

107

"Good point, Dad."

"Do tell," said Carol.

What, Gun thought, has happened to her?

"Adams mine fire of nineteen seventeen," Gunsten began. "September seventh, thirty men dead, Cornishmen, Poles, and of course Finns. There's a plaque up on Route Thirty-Five, and you can read about it and look at all the names." Gunsten seemed more expansive than usual, pleased to have this audience. "My dad was down there in shaft number four that day, twenty years old, two months married. All the way down on the seventeenth level, close to where it broke out. No one knows what started it burning, but men always liked to make fires to heat their tea at crib time, and the timbers on that level were reinforced with lagging—quite a few cords of it, real dry stuff— and that's what probably got it going so hot. Dad was lucky enough to get through the smoke and jump onto the skip, which the crew up top had kept running in case somebody had such a mind."

Gunsten leaned forward and rested one elbow on a knee. He narrowed his eyes, which over time had lost none of their pure blue power. "Those are the facts, Carol. Now here's the story."

Madilyn cleared her throat loudly and shifted on her chair. Gunsten ignored her. "The fire broke out, they said, about four in the afternoon. My dad didn't arrive at the surface until five-thirty. Now listen. He was working a hundred yards from the fire. Smoke from that fire killed men up to a quarter mile away. So how did he survive, you ask. Or look at it this way. Why did it take him so long—an hour and a half—to make the skip and ride to the top?" Gunsten was silent, his eyes throwing blue fire at Carol. She moved her face just barely and blinked, her quiet way of saying "I don't know."

"Well," said Gunsten, "all I can tell you is what he told me. He passed out on the floor of the stope, overcome by the smoke, he said. He was probably well on his way to dead, lying there unconscious for over an hour, the fire crashing away just a hundred yards off. The heat and smoke, think of it. And he's lying there like that when he hears my mother's voice tell him, 'Get up, Sonny.' That's what she always called him. 'Get yourself up now, I'm waiting.' And that's exactly what he did. Got himself up—from the dead, you might say—and out of there."

Carol shook her head. "Amazing."

"Gunsten's dad had a lot of them," said Madilyn.

"A true story," said Gunsten. "And I was born nine months later. Mom always said after Dad came up from the fire they got down to serious family business."

"I'm glad," said Carol. She turned ever so subtly toward Gun but didn't look at him.

"After that, seven kids in eight years," said Gunsten.

"That *is* serious," said Carol.

"I guess I was meant for this world," said Gunsten. He turned suddenly from Carol to Gun. "We've been talking today, your mother, Carol, and me. And we're sort of deciding things for you. Hope you don't object."

"Fill me in," said Gun.

Gunsten looked at his wife, as he often did when decisions had been reached and announcements were ready. As if she were the more worthy messenger, the one folks might listen to.

"This whole thing about Harry," said Madilyn. "Your father and I don't want you and Carol to throw off your plans." Madilyn swept her fingers back through her hair and rested the heels of her hands on

109

her temples in a gesture Gun recalled from an early memory: his mother, hair lit by a low morning sun, turning from the clothesline and staring across the yard at him; out of boredom Gun had just shattered a canning jar with a shot from his BB gun. Why was she giving him the same look now?

"Ah," said Gun. He saw Carol turn sharply from Madilyn to Gunsten and back again, eyebrows gathered.

"It's not fair to Carol," said Madilyn.

"I didn't set this up, Gun," Carol said. "We've just been talking is all. About what Hunter Watson had to say, the legal situation. There's not much of a case here. Not yet."

Gun leaned forward and took a bottle of blackberry soda from the bucket. His father tossed him an opener. "And we want to make sure it stays that way."

"Gun, at this point, what more can we do?" Carol's eyes ranged sympathetically toward Gun's father, who took a couple long swigs of soda, his bony Adam's apple jumping.

"Probably not much." Gun popped the metal cap from the soda bottle, lifted, and took a long swallow, thinking. Deciding. Then he sat for a moment enjoying the flavor before he said, "Which is why you and I are going to rise early tomorrow and leave for home, Carol. We'll have a couple of days to rest and pack and stare at corny travel brochures. How does that sound?"

Carol almost smiled but didn't. "A whole lot better than driving home and flying off alone, which is what I'd have done if you'd said otherwise."

"And don't think she's kidding," said Madilyn, rising from her chair. "Gunsten, you can help me get supper tonight."

The old man looked up at his wife. His bone-jutting,

leathery face acquiesced into a smile, but to maintain his pride he said, "I'm comfortable here."

"Then make yourself uncomfortable."

With a deep rumbling sigh Gunsten elbowed his way to his feet, stood tall, and offered an arm to his wife.

# 16

Gun got up from the lawn chair and lay down in the grass. He closed his eyes. In his chest and way out at the tips of his fingers he felt the warm tingling that came whenever he started to drift toward a badly needed sleep. The five o'clock sun burned warm and red through his eyelids, but the earth at his back still radiated the chill of winter.

Madilyn's soft laugh came floating out from the kitchen. Gun stole a peek at Carol and found himself being watched, though not with fondness, it seemed. "We'll have enough time," he said. "Get back tomorrow afternoon, and we don't fly out till Thursday. Then it's two weeks of sand." Gun tried to imagine this: fourteen days on the beach, the two of them alone together. The man whose villa they'd be renting, an old teammate of Gun's from Detroit, had told him the nights were cool. And Gun couldn't remember the last time he'd tasted island rum.

Carol hadn't turned away or blinked, and Gun felt her eyes inside his head now, pushing around the furniture.

"Don't say anything more," Carol said. "Please. We're leaving tomorrow. Those words are perfect, I want them to stand. I don't want to hear anything more."

"Not even—"

"Shhh." She lifted a finger to her lips.

Supper was shepherd's pie, everyone feeling easy at last, the conversation free of Harry Summers and even weddings. Gunsten questioned Carol on the finer points of running a weekly newspaper. They talked of reporting and of advertising rates, freedom of speech and the desktop publishing revolution. Afterward there was coffee and fresh-baked chocolate chip cookies in the screen gazebo Gunsten had put up in the backyard next to Madilyn's riotous flower garden. Carol invited Gun's parents to visit Minnesota in August, and Gunsten, normally a reluctant traveler, quickly accepted.

"Get a contract and a pen," said Madilyn.

"What's wrong with a man's word?" Standing, Gunsten laughed and said it was bedtime. "I don't guess I'll be up yet when the two of you leave in the morning. So good-bye. And have a nice wedding trip." Gun didn't rise for the farewell. He knew his dad would be up brewing coffee the minute the first pair of feet hit the floor in the morning.

"Good night," said Gunsten.

Madilyn stayed for another half hour, then got up to leave. Carol said she was tired, too. Gun watched the two as they went up toward the house. They were the same height, both moving with a slow young swing in their stride, and Gun smiled, marveling that every so often even *he* was capable of making a wise choice for himself. He lifted his hand from his leg and brought it knuckles-down against the wooden arm of the cedar chair.

It brought on a feeling that was too good to waste on sleep—watching these two women walking up the small rise toward the back door—and Gun held off for another forty-five minutes until his eyes started shutting him down against his will. He ate the last cookie from the plate, then got up and went into the house, careful to avoid the squeaky spots on the hardwood floor. His efforts were ruined by the telephone, which he got to before the second ring.

"Pedersens," he said quietly.

"Gunsten or Gun?" The voice was all air, a harsh whisper.

"Gun. Who am I talking to?"

"Somebody that's worried about you."

"Thanks."

"As it is," said the voice, "nobody in your family stands to lose anything, Gun." It sounded like a man, but Gun couldn't be sure. It was a whisper one might hear on a cheap, low-budget television movie about kidnaping. For a moment Gun almost felt like laughing.

"I think you should get on home, leave things alone. I think your efforts aren't much appreciated."

"By whom aren't they appreciated?" Gun asked.

"You been gone forever, Gun. You don't belong anymore. Now get the hell back to where you come from. Like I said, as it is, your family hasn't got anything to worry about." The line clicked, and the call was over.

Gun's stomach fisted up on him and pushed the chocolate chip cookies toward the bottom of his throat. He went to the kitchen sink and drank cold water from the tap. Then he looked around the kitchen, wishing for something to break, feeling inside the same rage he'd never learned to control during his years in baseball—phone calls from reporters quacking hearsay or begging quotes. And even that wasn't so bad if the guy gave his name. But when they didn't even have the balls to say who they were, that chewed on Gun's liver, kept him up nights.

He turned on the overhead light to think and sat down at the kitchen table. In his head he turned out a list. Green Tokannah, Myron and Mavis Summers, Calvin Summers, Neb Summers, all of them aware now that Gun was serious about getting to bedrock on Harry's death. And what about Harry's great uncle in Toronto? What did he know? And Dandrie? Did he matter at all? What sort of grip did he have on Calvin Summers?

Right now Gun knew just one thing for sure. In the last day or so he'd gotten a little too close to the truth for somebody's liking.

The chances of getting any sleep were lousy as a dog dead three days in the ditch, and to put his anger to use Gun decided to go for a drive. It was only ten-thirty and nothing coming from upstairs but quiet.


Neb Summers and his wife Nora lived on the north edge of Copper Strike in what had been the Quincy General Store, a place where as a boy Gun had spent his summer money on Popsicles and baseball cards. That business, along with many others, had gone belly-up in '69 when the last of the mines had closed. Neb and Nora bought it cheap a year later, and for a long time Nora sold rummage and old furniture on the main floor. Now, according to Madilyn, with Neb sick Nora didn't have time to make the rounds of auctions and estate sales.

Tonight the building was lit up. Two cars, one of them Calvin's, were parked out front.

Nora came to the door. She was short and trim, her well-tended gray hair cut close on the sides and swept back from her forehead.

"Gun," she said, pushing open the screen door; she seemed less than happy to see him.

"Nora, everyone else I know is getting older."

She smiled and looked down at herself. She had on an aqua nylon running suit and Rocsport walkers. "Thanks, Gun. I probably work a little too hard too hide the fact that I am, too."

"Is Neb home?"

Nora ushered him inside. The large main floor still looked more like a store than a home, a single, high-ceilinged room with an age-darkened wood floor. The plaster walls were covered with elaborately framed Audubons and Currier and Ives. Antique desks, bureaus, chifferobes, and tables stood in groupings that made no sense to Gun's eye. He followed Nora to the northwest corner of the building, where, behind a massive ebony hutch, Neb, Calvin, and a man Gun didn't recognize were sitting drinking coffee around an old pool table. Nora left Gun with the men, saying, "I'll bring you a cup."

"Kind of late, Gun. Something wrong?" Neb was haggard, the skin of his face like paper corrugated by rain, no flesh underneath to give it form.

"As a matter of fact, yes." Gun looked around the table. Calvin seemed chastened after last night. His eyes met Gun's, but with humble curiosity. The third man made Gun think of a large cat, the way he sat: relaxed yet alert, muscular energy rolling off him. His hair was like spring wire and Gun suddenly remembered—he'd been with Henry's parents at the memorial service.

"You probably don't know Rufus," said Neb. "Calvin's cousin, Harry's, too. Lives in Chicago. He came over for the memorial service. My sister's boy. You remember Pearl, Gun."

Gun nodded, though all he recalled of Pearl was the stunned face she wore in the presence of her husband Jim, a Copper Strike miner who'd never recovered from the motorcycle crash that put him on permanent disability.

"Pearl and Jim are both dead now," Neb said. "Cancer." He spoke the word slowly, with hateful respect.

"I'm sorry." Gun looked at Rufus, whose eyes slid up carefully, met Gun's, and darted away. He fingered a cigarette from a pack of Marlboros. His hands were large and graceful.

"You were saying . . ." Neb said to Gun, then he stopped himself as Nora arrived with a cup of coffee and a glass pot for refills. Gun had a taste and offered a compliment. Nora moved off. The three men kept their eyes on Gun. No one spoke for a few moments. No one moved. The air was tight with waiting.

Gun was feeling perverse, in the mood to draw this tension out. He said, "Rufus, what do you do for a living?"

The man looked square into Gun's eyes now and drew back his lips in a joyless smile. His teeth were perfectly straight and dotted with gold. "Repo work. Tracking down vehicles and taking them back," said Rufus. "Sometimes a guy shows up at the wrong time." His smile flared up a little.

"Yeah, that's the part Rufus likes," said Calvin. He seemed overly impressed.

"Sounds like fun," Gun said.

"I ain't rich yet."

Gun turned back to Neb. "I told you I'd keep you

posted on what I'm learning, and I guess I learned something tonight—though I'm not sure what. I got a phone call."

"Who from?"

"Caller wouldn't say. Suggested I go on home and quit asking questions."

"When did you get the call?"

"Fifteen minutes ago."

"And you ran right over *here?*"

Gun looked around the table again. He sensed all three men just dying for the chance to deny something. Okay, then, he thought. The fist tightened in his stomach. He said, "Calvin here's been less than accommodating, Neb. And I have to say it strikes me that you're not exactly breaking your butt on this case. Like the way you took Green Tokannah's word straight to the bank. It doesn't sit right with me, Neb. Makes me wonder."

"Makes you wonder what?"

"You're the law, Neb. You tell me."

One of Calvin's big shoulders jerked, and he cleared something out of his sinuses. He was looking hard into his coffee.

"Shut up, Calvin," said Neb.

"I didn't say nothing."

"You should've," said Rufus. "God, the trembling flesh here. Some guy comes around to my place and talks like that—"

"Shut up, Rufus."

"I'm not shootin' you down, Uncle Neb. You've got cancer, that's different. But your kid here. This guy comes around, I don't care if he played in a hundred all-star games, pointing his finger, and goddamn, it's his old man for all we know that put Harry away, and Calvin *sits* here with his fat thumbs up his rear end. I'm gonna be sick."

118

Gun watched as Calvin cranked his head to one side, then the other, his neck cracking like a set of practiced knuckles. He was looking at Rufus's chest, no higher, when he spoke. "Nobody talks to me that way that knows me. Which you do, Rufus."

"I do, pal, and the fact we're related is what makes it all the more embarrassing sitting here. Who's got hold of your balls, Calvin?"

Calvin stood up fast, his stool flying backward to the floor, and he threw one long arm across the pool table. Rufus didn't move but glanced down at Calvin's fist, which had closed around his shirt collar.

"That's it now, boys," said Neb, but his command was weak.

"Get outta here, Dad."

"Leave, Uncle Neb," said Rufus.

Neb got off his stool and started moving away, saying, "Watch it, now, that's good slate, and original felt, too, and I sure paid for it."

Gun sat and watched, feeling left out. Calvin and Rufus were locked together at the eyes and screwed down tight. They were leaning toward each other, green felt-covered table between them, Calvin's reaching arm taut and corded, his fist like a red knobby stone beneath his cousin's chin. Rufus laughed and took a grip on Calvin's forearm. Gun heard cloth tear as Rufus broke Calvin's grip on his collar, then muscled Calvin's arm all the way down to the felt. He smiled and let go. For a space of seconds it was over, then Calvin's hand rose in a blur and slapped Rufus on the cheek twice—backhand, forehand—and Rufus was over the table, his shoulder colliding with Calvin's chest and riding it to the floor, his fist pumping up and down half a dozen times before Gun could get there and knock Rufus clear with a knee to the ribs.

Calvin's nose lay flaccid against one cheek, and blood ran into his eyes and down into his mouth. "I'll get ice," Gun said. Calvin's fingers explored his face, panicky, like rats on a pile of freshly spilled grain.

Gun was beginning to rise when he took the blow on the side of his head, falling when he felt Rufus's knee paralyze the big front thigh muscle of his right leg, then everything in the room was orange, even the boot coming for Gun's face. He ducked, took the blow with the hard top of his cranium, and made a sideways dive for sanctuary beneath the pool table. On the way another boot found him, this time in the crotch. Not a direct hit, but bad enough to make his stomach rise sick into his throat and his jaw start shooting the panic juices. Instinct and nausea told him to roll himself tight under the table and wait this out. He acted instead on his rage, which had the blood roaring in his neck and his eyes somewhere outside himself, watching as he got his feet on the floor, his shoulders braced against the bottom of the slate. The big table was weightless and crashed back against the wall, slate snapping and creaking. He saw himself take a left hook to the cheekbone, absorb it like his nerves weren't home, a straight right hand to the stomach, it, too—and then he was grabbing Rufus, the man's face slick with concern, his eyes set for the pain Gun dealt him now, grabbing him almost lovingly by the denim shirt front, so pleased to have this opportunity, lifting him off the floor and throwing his body headfirst into the wrecked table.

Rufus hit the table with force, the back of his shoulders taking most of the blow, but he was on his feet immediately. Gun told him to sit. Rufus sat, relieved, it seemed, one arm falling loosely over an upthrust tableleg. His breath was coming in quick gusty swallows and coughs, but his face looked extremely happy. He said, "Wow, great."

Calvin was still on the floor, cradling his head in his hands, and when he spoke it was in a pinched voice through his altered nose. "You're a sweet guy, Rufus."

"You're a pussy, Calvin."

Neb peeked around the corner of the large hutch, his flesh-eaten face wagging back and forth.

"Sorry about the table," Gun said. The surge of adrenaline had gone and left him feeling drugged and stupid. He had to think for a moment to find his reason for even being here. "Who do you suppose it is, Neb, that doesn't want me poking around?"

"You gonna pay me for the table?" Neb asked.

"No." Gun touched his fingers to his cheek to assess damage, felt a bruise thickening there. "Are *you* the one getting nervous, Neb?"

"You are, Pedersen," said Calvin. "And hey, if your old man was my old man, I'd be as bad off as you are."

Neb's wife appeared suddenly with her coffeepot steaming, and Neb tried to send her away. But she remained, standing there in her gym outfit, chin aimed at her husband. "This is how we welcome an old friend to our home?" Her eyes sliced away all possibility of argument. Neb scratched his nose. Nora looked in disgust at the overturned table, at her son, at Rufus. She said, "You know how long we've known Gun? Let me tell you. I remember him hitting a ball through the library window at school. He couldn't have been more than eight or nine. I was up there working on math, and I picked up the ball and threw it back outside. I was a junior in high school. . . ."

"He comes in here talking—"

"That's enough, Rufus. This is my house, and you're in it. I'll toss you out on your ass." She took a breath, collecting herself, then reached out and put a flat hand on her husband's chest. "Neb, I heard Gun ask you a question. Are you going to answer it?"

"No answer to give," said Neb, shaking his head. His face looked bad, everything pouched and sagging. "None," he said.

Gun thanked Nora for the coffee and left.

# 17

She lay there in a soft crescent of moonlight, her face composed in sleep like a child's face. The blanket that covered her was a patchwork quilt Gun's grandmother had made for him long ago. Carol lay on her stomach, one knee drawn close to her rib cage, her elbows fanned out like small wings. For a pillow she used a forearm. Her breathing made no sound at all, but Gun could see the slight rise and fall of her back.

Quietly he picked up a small chair from the desk by the window, set it next to the bed, and sat down to watch her. He felt he owed Carol a second consideration, a chance to let her loveliness change his mind, or at least try. Of course, once he'd wakened her and said the words out loud she would dismiss further discussion. He knew this absolutely. You do what you're going to do, she'd say, and this response would both anger and please Gun. It was part of why he loved her—her strength, her unwillingness to make appeals on her own behalf. It was also why he could think to walk away at a time like this.

He watched her now, studied her lips, which were still full at forty, the upper one with its perfect double point—the sort most women had to paint on in front of the mirror. He reached out and touched Carol's face, waking her, then stayed quiet as her eyes gained focus and brightened. She turned toward him but did not lift her head.

"What time is it?" she asked.

"Late . . . almost two." Gun had left Neb's about eleven and driven all the way up to Copper Harbor, where he'd stood on the sand beach watching the dark waters that at some not-so-distant point became Canadian.

Carol was alert now and reading Gun's mind—ransacking it. There was no surprising Carol, ever, no saving something for later. It wasn't fair. He said, "Don't look at me that way."

"You don't deserve it?"

"No." He'd decided not to tell her about the phone call or the ruckus over at Neb's. He didn't want to seem defensive—it was the wrong tone to strike. He didn't want to be trapped into discussing the validity of his reasons, and he knew she wouldn't start pushing if he didn't open the door. He said, "I can't go back home like I said. Not just yet."

"All right," she said, her voice flat and final.

He felt pleased at her response, then instant shame for being pleased. "I'd be letting him down . . . my dad."

"We can't have that." Again, nothing at all in Carol's voice.

"No, we can't," said Gun evenly.

"How much longer do you need?" Carol asked.

"Couple more days. I need to go up to Toronto, visit with a guy. It's better if I don't put it off."

"All right."

"I drove around for a couple hours tonight, went up to the lake. I let it all sift down. . . .This isn't easy for me, either."

"Have you talked with your dad?"

"Nope."

Carol was still looking into him, and he felt as if she'd managed somehow to strip every shred of motive and intent from every brain cell he owned. He said, "I feel like a bastard doing this. I'm sorry, Carol."

She shrugged, and one shoulder slipped out from beneath the old quilt. He reached out and smoothed his hand across her skin. It was warm, almost moist. He imagined its saltiness. He said, "I don't want you to take it the wrong way."

"What do you mean?"

"I mean, leaving like this—it doesn't change anything, as far as I'm concerned. We'll just have to put off the wedding for a week or two."

Carol was shaking her head. "Apparently you didn't hear me tonight, Gun. I said if you're not going back now, fine, but I *am*. And I'm going to use my airline ticket, too. And the hotel reservation."

Gun stood up and moved the chair back to the desk. He could already feel the miles stretching out between them but didn't allow himself any regret. "Okay," he said. "Then have a nice honeymoon."

At the bedroom door he turned to look back. Her eyes were closed.

# 18

The only paper Gun could find in the kitchen was a white bakery bag from the stack in the broom closet, wedged in next to the flour bin. Apparently on those days when Gunsten had paying work that took him away Madilyn still packed noon lunches. Bratwurst or summer sausage or cheese, no doubt, on home-baked white bread. For dessert, oatmeal cookies or a fat piece of pie wrapped in wax paper.

Gun sat down at the table and scratched out a note. He was off to Toronto for a couple days, he wrote, and Carol would need a lift to Houghton first thing in the morning; she'd be needing to rent a car for the trip back to Minnesota. "Don't worry," he added, "I know what I'm doing," this last phrase, though necessary, sounding pathetically false even to him. Driving out of the yard, he looked up at his parents' second-story bedroom window and saw the large white head of his father.

Marquette was a two-hour drive, which Gun survived thanks to the bag of baby carrots lifted from his ' mother's crisper. The crunching kept him going despite his body's all-out lobby for sleep. He felt sections of his body go numb and disappear: his left thigh, right hand, his scalp. At the airport he slept for two hours sitting more or less upright in a hard plastic chair, then he stole another hour in the 727. By the time he stepped off the plane at Toronto's Pearson airport, sensation had returned to his skin. Two cups of coffee from an airport cafeteria brought him close to par, and a surprisingly fresh pastry stuffed with cream cheese finished the job.

Outside he flagged a Diamond taxi, asked for downtown, then watched Lake Ontario spread out before him to the south as they drove down through the City of Etobicoke on 427. The water this morning was calm, a dull blue-green prairie beneath heavy skies. They entered downtown on the Gardiner Expressway during rush hour, and Gun had more opportunity than he cared for to observe the recent alterations of Toronto's skyline. He hadn't been here since 1980, his last season with the Tigers. In the passing decade the city fathers had thrown a lot of glass and concrete into the air above the harbor.

Gun's first glimpse of the Skydome didn't bring shivers or thrills. It was hunkered down beneath the CN Tower, a giant bloated curiosity with just enough swoop in it to suggest a Jetsons cartoon. In Gun's day the Blue Jays had been a fledgling team that played bad baseball beneath obnoxious seagulls at old Exhibition Stadium. Times had changed. The franchise was coming off its first World Series victory after years of being the American League's frustrated bridesmaid. They looked good again this year, too, though they'd lost some punch when Winfield went to Minnesota.

Stepping from the cab and looking around, he found himself at King and Yonge streets. Half a block away stood the King Edward Hotel, where the Tigers had stayed on road trips. A first-class place with good food and lots of marble, Gun remembered.

Though he'd decided to find a phone booth and call Max Summers right away, now he saw his own image in the tinted window of a tobacco shop and changed his mind. He was unshaven, with exhausted eyes. His face was slack from fatigue, his hair oily and flat to his skull. He walked into King Eddie's and got himself a room from a young clerk—blond, toothy, and well-groomed—who seemed unconvinced that Gun's American Express card was any good, even after the customary phone check.

An hour later, after a short nap and long shower, Gun stood wrapped in a towel before a gold-framed mirror. He was vastly improved. A dozen years younger. His short white hair was back to its normal unruliness, his shoulders and eyes out there where you could see them again. He wondered how he'd look to Diane, reminded himself that he wouldn't be seeing her, then put on his travel-smelling shirt and pants and left the hotel. At a men's store a block north he bought a pair of chinos, clean underwear and socks, and a fresh white shirt. He paid for them, then put them on in a dressing room, where he left his old clothes in a pile on the floor for someone to find and throw away.

The Toronto subway, just as clean as he remembered it, took him thirty blocks east to the address he'd gotten out of the phone book. Max Summers's neighborhood was faded though still handsome, European in its closely plotted townhomes of brick and stone, narrow streets quaint beneath the green tent of aging maples.

The old man answered the door only after Gun had knocked for five minutes and was about to give up. He was bent, though still rather tall. He wore glasses that magnified his one good snapping-blue eye to golf ball–size proportions. The other eye was covered by a leather patch. "How come you don't knock?" he asked.

"I did, for quite a while."

"Lucky I was up to go pee, or I wouldn't have spotted you out the window."

"My name is Gun Pedersen." Gun put out his hand, and they shook.

"Max Summers. Who're you?"

"Gun Pedersen, I said. A friend of your nephew Myron's." Gun was yelling now, though he tried to seem as if he weren't.

The big blue eye narrowed into a moist black seed, and Max Summers stuck a finger into an ear. "Wait," he said. He retreated a few steps to a dark bureau and plucked up a flesh-colored hearing aid, an old wrap-around-the-ear style. "Now"—he fixed the device into his ear—"who are you?"

Gun told him again.

"So you must be here about Harry."

Gun nodded. Max Summers took him by the elbow and led him into the next room. With the help of a cane Max sat himself down carefully on a stuffed Victorian chair. Gun pulled the matching chair close and sat down facing the man. The room was small and light, floor-to-ceiling bookcases on two walls, high windows to the east and south. On a small dark table was propped a grouping of yellowed photographs in black metal frames: men in uniform, World War I. A vintage helmet sat next to the photographs.

Max said, "No need for small talk. Doubt you're here for that." He smiled. "But if you want, you could

# L. L. ENGER

go into the kitchen there and turn on the water for tea.
Pot's full."

Gun obliged him and came back. "Did somebody
call and tell you I'd be coming?"

"Not exactly."

"You're not surprised I'm here, though."

"No." Max Summers's voice was throaty and
harsh, a barking bird. It reminded Gun of the sound
pheasants make, hiding out in the undergrowth.

"Why not?"

The old man had settled deep into his chair. His
build was narrow, and he sat leaning forward with his
two hands wrapped around the top of his cane, which
was planted between his slippered feet. He shrugged
and blinked his eye. "'Course I heard from just about
everybody when they found him. They all knew how
much Harry meant to me. We used to go fishing, the
two of us, every summer when he was a little guy.
Then later, when he was a not-so-little guy, too. I
probably got along better with that boy than his own
dad did. My guess is that Myron's wife mentioned my
name, said you oughta talk to me."

"Yeah." Gun leaned back to give the man's mind
and memory room to expand.

"She always had Harry riding around inside of her.
Still does, I'd guess. Myron, he only sees what he
wants to, like most of the Summers men. Like most
men. But I'm different." He closed his eye, thought for
a moment. "Comes from never having a son of my
own. Not having to go around trying to duplicate
myself. A father blinds himself out of necessity. Do
you have sons?"

In the kitchen the teapot started whistling, and Gun
rose to take care of it. "Cups are in the right-hand
cupboard, middle shelf, tea bags on the counter," said
Max Summers.

Gun called out, "Sugar?"

"There in that peach dish," Max said. The sugar bowl was made of pottery shaped like a peach and glazed to a burnt shade of yellow-orange. Everything in the house, Gun noticed, was of impeccable taste, and well cared for. Gun brought the tea and set it on the small table between the chairs.

"No," said Gun. "One daughter's all I've got, and that was hard enough."

"I have three of those. Sweet girls. Perfect. Raised themselves up like nothing, as if they hardly needed me." Max Summers tried his tea and nodded.

"Are you still married?" Gun asked.

"My wife died two years ago this spring. Daughter lives next door. She's the reason for this." Max Summers reached out and wiped a finger across the bookcase to his left. He held up the finger for Gun to see. It was clean.

Gun said, "Why did Mavis think I should talk to you?"

The old man laughed. "As I said, I was close to Harry, and so was she. The difference is, she lives down there, among the Summerses. Myron, Neb, Calvin, all of them. I live up here alone—separated from the family. So there are things she can't say and I can say."

"What things?" Gun asked.

"I've got to back up just a bit. I won't make this long for you, Pedersen, but I want you to understand the situation—and understand me, too. I have my pride." He leaned forward to bite the knuckles of his hand. His lips were thin and moved as if controlled by a drawstring cord, puckering tight. He was still leaning on the cane. "The Summerses are a military family, as I'm sure you know. My father fought in Cuba with Teddy Roosevelt. My grandfather knew Stonewall Jackson. You see, we're transplanted from the south originally. Tennessee." Max Summers's blue eye

**131**

found Gun and shone on him. "Those that came after me, listen: Neb and Myron had Korea. Calvin, Vietnam. But what about old Max, you're thinking. What's the geezer doing up here in Toronto? Did he run? Well, let me tell you. I'm up here on foreign land because my country wouldn't have me when it came time for *my* war. I turned eighteen in eighteen, perfect timing. Lots of trenches just waiting for me over there. Trouble was, I only had this one headlight here"—he pointed to his eye. "Lost the other to the family milk cow, which happened to go crazy one morning when I was eight years old. So the U.S. Army said Sorry, Max, and I heard the Canadians needed ambulance drivers, so up I came. Of course, everybody knows the story about young Hemingway, who did the same thing—came up here, signed on, eventually got himself shot up in Italy. Made a career of it, too. Didn't know the man personally, so don't ask me about him."

Max took a deep breath and then some tea. A drop of it rolled from the corner of his mouth to the tip of his chin, but he didn't seem to notice. "I didn't get shot up like the writer," he went on, "but I did find a wife. A Torontonian. I met her right off, before they even shipped me to Milan. We wrote back and forth, then found a preacher when I got back. A good wife, too, she was, but she wouldn't stand for leaving Toronto, and I wouldn't stand for leaving her—so . . . seventy years later, here I am."

Max Summers finished his cup of tea, then reached into the breast pocket of his shirt and pulled out a lemon drop, which he popped into his mouth. "You live a distance from your family like I've done, you get some insights. I'm talking personal *and* political. Might be the fact I was up here in Toronto, too, but when you guys were doing your bit against communism in Vietnam it looked pretty bloody futile to me. Pretty dumb, too. Not that I didn't hate the communists—and I'm no pacifist, or anything like that. I just didn't see the point. Like trying to kill off the whole ant colony by raiding one little picnic." He wagged a finger in the air. "Now be patient. The subject is Harry Summers, and what you probably don't know is that Harry felt a whole lot like I did about that war. I didn't preach at him, either. Just listened to the boy. When I heard him talking sense I told him if he ever needed a place to get away, I'd have that place for him. And *that*, I'm here to tell you, is not something I would've mentioned to Neb or Myron."

"You're saying Harry was planning to come up here? Jump the draft?"

"I'm saying it wouldn't have surprised me. He never said he was coming or wasn't, but I do know he got a draft notice that summer, and I was thinking I might see him."

"You didn't, though."

"I didn't."

"After he turned up missing did anybody come looking? Anybody give you a call?"

Max Summers shook his head. "Nobody would've thought to, except Mavis, probably. See, if Harry planned to run, he sure as damnation wouldn't have been talking about it. Not to his family."

"What if he did talk, though?" Gun asked.

"You're saying would somebody have killed him for wanting to run? I sure don't like to think so." Max looked away from Gun toward window, blinked at the white glare of the sun. "No," he said.

"But Mavis never called? You're sure of that."

"Oh, she called. Never came right out and asked any questions, I guess, but she gave me plenty of chances to talk." Max reached out and took hold of a framed photograph from the table, held it out for Gun

to see. "That's me there in the front row, far left."
Young Max didn't look much different from old Max.
He'd been skinny then, too. Same narrow mouth, nose
and cheeks a bit fuller, no glasses. A look of pride in
the bones of his face.

"You never put Mavis's mind at ease?" Gun asked.
"Told her you didn't know anything?"

"For all I knew, Harry was up here somewhere. I
didn't want to kill a mother's hopes." Max blew on
the glass-covered photograph and propped it back up
on the table. He looked at Gun and shook his head.
"Maybe it wasn't the right thing I did. But the
easiest."

They were quiet for minute. The sun from the front
window had reached Gun's knee, warming it. He said,
"Do you know of any trouble Harry might've been in
that summer? Any theories of your own about what
happened?"

"Harry was never in trouble, that's for sure. People
loved him, he loved people . . . and baseball." Max
shook his head and tossed one bony hand in the air.
His leather-slippered feet shuffled against the polished
maple.

"Hard to believe you don't even have a hunch, close
as you and Harry were."

Max studied Gun for a moment before saying,
quietly, "You're up here for hunches?"

"You bet I am," Gun said.

"All right." Max's single blue iris was as hard and
clear as a cat's-eye marble. "But keep in mind that's
what this is. No more."

Gun nodded, waited.

"I got a call three days ago, from Neb. Which by
itself is very unusual. Nora's the one that makes
contact if it's necessary. Neb and I . . . well, there's
not much to talk about. Never has been. He called a
day or two after I heard about Harry. See, both Nora

and Myron had called earlier with the bad news. When I heard Neb on the line I figured it was something about the funeral—not that I was planning on being there. I'm too old for that trip. But Neb had something else on his mind. Money. He needed some and figured I had it."

"He wanted a loan?"

"Fifty thousand dollars," said Max, smiling. "Now I've lent money to family before. Myron once, and Calvin a couple times. He never pays me back. But fifty grand?"

"What'd he say he needed it for? Medical expenses?"

"I doubt it. Everything I hear, that insurance Neb gets working for the city covers it all. I didn't ask, though. He sounded bad enough without having to explain himself. He didn't try, either."

"Did you give it to him?"

"Not what he asked for, by a long shot. But I sent him a check. He sounded bad off . . . what am I gonna do?"

"What about this hunch of yours?" Gun asked.

Max Summers's head shot up from his small shoulders. His neck was turkeylike, loose skin and taut cords. He scowled. "You're the one that used the word *hunch,* not me."

Gun agreed and waited.

"Neb's call, coming when it did, just made me think is all. It doesn't make any sense, and I sure don't have anything to base it on. Just a feeling I've got." Max popped another lemon drop into his mouth. "I'm tired. Ninety-three years old and I was up at four this morning. Couldn't sleep. Now it's time for my nap." He leaned forward heavily on his cane, as if to stand.

"I need to hear what's on your mind about Neb," Gun said, "no matter how it sounds."

The old man nodded and leaned back in the chair

again, took a breath and let it out like a horse through flapping lips. "Neb and Nora got together right after the war. They met one night in a dance hall, got married the next day. Fast and hot. The sort of couple you don't want to be around too much, kissing, rubbing up against each other in public. You understand? They might forget where they are and take their clothes off. My God, the moves that woman could make." Max aimed his eye at Gun, giving his words some time to work. Gun nodded.

"This went on for years after the honeymoon. Years. This is abnormal, Pedersen. The spring before Harry disappeared they had a family reunion down there, and it was embarrassing. Two middle-aged folks acting like kids with hormones. Then it changed, all of a sudden. And Neb and Nora weren't the same. In fact, she moved out on him that fall. Moved back, of course, but whatever good they had up till then was gone. I asked Nora what happened, but she wouldn't say. It wasn't much later she spent a few months in the mental hospital. You know about that?"

"Rings a bell," Gun said.

"Nervous breakdown, they said, but I've talked to Nora from time to time over the years, and she strikes me as rock-solid sane. Don't know what happened to her, but I'd say she's recovered. Her and Neb, though, they haven't."

Max sat forward and leaned once more on his cane. "Like I said, I don't know why, but getting that call from Neb last week, and him wanting money? It got me wondering again about what happened to Neb and Nora the summer Harry disappeared." He shook his head and rubbed water from his eye. "All I know for sure is I need my nap." He pushed himself to his feet. "See? I told you it wouldn't make any sense. That'll teach you to sit with an old man."

Gun stood, too. "When I get back I'll look up Nora," he said, feeling little hope.

Max moved toward the front entrance, punching his cane on the wood floor. "Catch her when Neb's not around." He drew open the door for Gun. "Tell her I'm wondering what happened to the moves she used to have."

# 19

*B*reakfast was scrambled eggs and ham in a little working-class café full of cab drivers on Bathurst and College, a place Gun had discovered with Jack Morris in '79. A morning after a night game in which Morris had gone nine two-hit innings only to lose one-nothing.

Gun drank coffee and stewed. He thought of Max Summers, and the old man's memories of Neb and Nora, love they'd had and lost. He thought of Diane Apple, right here somewhere in this same city and found himself getting angry at Carol. He thought of the conversation he'd had with Hunter Watson and how in a case like this one—twenty-five-year-old bones and a murderous hammer—a man might win his battle in court and still lose everything he's worked for in his life, everything he stands for. Never mind due process.

Gun imagined his father at this moment. Sweating

through a long sauna. Riding somewhere on the Indian. Cutting through swells on Lake Superior, throttling wide open and standing straight at the wheel, head clear of the windshield, white hair streaming.

Outside the window of the café Gun saw a man arguing with a constable who was writing out a parking violation. The man's face was red, not from anger but from sun and weather. He wore overalls, a flannel shirt, and a green feed cap. The vehicle getting the ticket was a seventies model Dodge truck, rusty. The constable shook his head and walked off. The man climbed heavily into his truck and drove away.

This trip, Gun realized, had likely been a waste of time. He had expected the great uncle to have something more concrete, at least a solid hunch. Foolishly, he'd thought that Myron's wife, despite the disturbed state of her mind, had sent him in the right direction. So here he was, sitting useless in Toronto, while Carol drove west through Wisconsin, no doubt convinced in her own mind that Gun, after all, was not the man with whom she could negotiate life.

At least the coffee was good, heavy-flavored yet not bitter, and Gun let the waitress fill his cup yet again. He felt like a hitter up to bat in the ninth inning, two outs and trailing by half a dozen runs. He told himself not to cave in. Asked himself what he was able to do *now*. The answers weren't long in coming. Go back to Michigan and talk with Nora. Find out if, in fact, there was something she wanted or needed to tell. Scratch around, learn what he could about Dandrie and his connection to Calvin Summers. Give Carol a call and persuade her not to give up on him. Yet about this resolution, Gun was not certain. In truth, he wondered if he had already given up on her. Last night, watching her face harden there in the upstairs bedroom of his parents' home, something sharp inside him had turned, and he wondered if it could ever be turned back again.

He paid his check and walked outside. The day was humid and warming fast, approaching uncomfortable. He spotted a taxi and waved. The taxi didn't even slow. He was watching for another when a voice said, "I warned you about coming near me again." It was a warm voice, coming to him from a shaft of sweet memories.

# 20

*A*rms crossed in front of her, Reeboked feet spaced apart and planted unequivocally on the sidewalk, she stood there like an impossibly beautiful third-base coach. The pale gray tint of grief was gone from her face and she was tan now, a slight reddish burn on her forehead and cheeks. Her long heavy auburn hair had been chopped at the shoulders, and her eyes were wide, curious, yet sharp with purpose.

All Gun could say was, "Hello."

"Hello."

"You're . . . here," he said stupidly.

"So are you." She stepped toward him then. Her sudden closeness and the soapy smell of her freed him from his awkwardness. Her palms pressed his back for a moment, then she pushed away. She looked up. "But you're not here to see me," she said.

"I'm not sure."

She was holding one of his hands but now let go of it. "Did you get my letter last fall?" There was hurt in her face, but she smiled to cover it.

Gun nodded. He didn't try to explain.

"So then . . . you know what I'm doing in Toronto."

"Yeah, yeah." He took a breath and knew how good he felt, just looking at her again. "Are they treating it right?" he asked. In her letter she'd said her script had been taken by Tri-Star Pictures. A baseball film. It was the break she'd been working years for.

"Hard to say right now. I'm new at this. But you haven't said why *you're* here."

"Visiting an old man. Somebody who has, um, some business with my father."

"You make it sound intriguing."

"I guess it is."

"You do have a way of involving yourself in certain kinds of situations," said Diane. She pushed a hand back through her hair, and Gun's memory gave him a quick glimpse of the moment he'd first seen her: sitting there in the dim cabin of her brother's boat, bare feet up on the table, hair done in a long, thick braid that rested heavily on one shoulder, her sad, wonderfully boned face soft where it should be, in the lips and eyes.

"There's a shoot scheduled for one o'clock I don't want to miss," Diane said. "In the Skydome. Come with me."

Gun heard, beneath his own silence, the blood coursing through his ears. He said, "All right," louder than necessary.

In the cab he gave her some background—the discovery of Harry's body, his father's keys and hammer, Neb Summers's attitude. Diane mostly listened and made sympathetic sounds. Gun didn't mention Carol Long, but he couldn't stay away from her in his mind.

At the Skydome Diane flashed a security pass, then she and Gun were ushered inside and onto the playing field. The retractable dome was in place; rain must be in the forecast. In front of the first-base dugout, with its stainless-steel cuspidors complete with running water, Gun did a slow three-sixty, his face turned toward the amazing rise of empty seats and sky boxes. He experienced a touch of vertigo. What he'd read and seen on television had not prepared him for the vastness of this park.

"Unbelievable place," Diane said. "See up there?" She pointed toward huge glass windows high above the outfield. "You can get a hotel room, watch the game from bed. Thousand bucks a night. And there" —she aimed her finger toward a spot above right field—"that's the Hard Rock Café. They've also got a running track up there, goes all the way around at roof level. Complete health club. Seven bars and restaurants."

"You should do a commercial."

"I'll admit I'm impressed. Of course, I'm not a ballplayer."

"Yeah, I guess they do some baseball here, too."

"You can see where they're setting up, down there along the bullpen." She nodded toward the third-base side of the field. "This scene today, there's a conversation between the hero—an aging pitcher trying to come back after surgery—and a woman in the stands. She's the love interest. He's warming up late in the game when they meet. She calls out to him from her seat, tells him what's wrong with his delivery. He tries out her advice, and presto."

"Sounds realistic," Gun said.

"It's a movie," said Diane, a little defensive. "And I think it'll work."

"Who's got the part of the pitcher?"

"Nobody you've heard of. And the girl's new, too. We're not talking large budget here, Gun, but they did get Hackman for a character role. You want to walk over and watch?"

"Just a second." He nodded toward a tall man with dark hair and an untrimmed mustache who was crossing the first-base line. "Here comes somebody I know."

The man wore a gray sweatsuit, and a glove dangled from his left index finger.

"If it ain't the hermit himself. What the hell'd you do now, Pedersen—give up the woods for acting?"

"Hey, Luke." They shook hands. Luke Masters had been with Detroit during Gun's last couple of years, and now, pushing forty, he was coming off the best year of his career. He was in the Blue Jays' rotation and already had eight wins.

Gun introduced him to Diane Apple, who received from Luke Masters the smile he'd always saved for pretty women—a quick flash of the eye, a slight curl in the upper lip. "Scriptwriter, huh?" the pitcher said.

Diane nodded, evidently unimpressed. Luke shrugged and turned to Gun.

"Must be some job," Gun said, "keeping up with the boys after all these years."

"Nah, easy." He winked.

"Ryan's still going. Blyleven."

"I love the work," said Luke, smiling. "How about you?"

"I'm up here on business. Diane's a friend. Happened to run into her." Gun let his words drop in a way that didn't invite questions. "Are you involved in the film?" he asked.

Luke laughed. "The actors they got never played a day of ball in their lives. They hired me to teach a guy how to *look* like he knows how to throw. Pain in the ass. Good money." He nodded toward a young man walking to the mound, suited up and looking pleased with himself, long strides, chest thrown forward.

"And see that guy?" Luke pointed to another young man shifting dirt around with his toe in the batter's box. "They've got Kelly Wilson teaching him how to *look* like he knows how to hit." Wilson, third baseman for the Jays, carried all-star offensive numbers and a glove to boot. "Speaking of Wilson, he's supposed to be here," Luke said.

The guy on the mound glanced over. "Keep your shorts on," Luke called to him. He turned to Gun. "You want to give some pointers to the kid at the plate?"

"Why not?"

Diane said, "I've gotta get over to the shoot."

"I'll wander by in a few minutes," Gun told her.

The actor who was supposed to hit was ball-shy and kept bailing out, even when Luke softened up to softball speed. "Keep your lead foot on a line toward the pitcher when you stride," Gun told him. "Don't step toward third base. He's not gonna hit you."

"That's Luke Masters out there—God," said the actor. His dark hair was fashionably long in back, and Gun supposed the stubble on his chin was meant to create big-league authenticity.

A Toronto batboy was rounding up the balls, which in the absence of a catcher were hitting the dirt and bounding back to the screen.

"Here," Gun said, "I'll swat a few, and you watch." He wasn't feeling instructive so much as he wanted to feel the sensation of hitting a live ball again. The hitting machine back home made for good practice but not much excitement.

Gun asked the batboy for something bigger, and the kid brought him a thirty-five-incher, narrow handle. Just right. Gun made himself comfortable, digging a little hole for his right foot, waving the meat of the stick over the plate, shifting his weight to the back foot. He told himself to keep his front shoulder in and told Luke, "Keep it interesting."

The pitcher laughed and swung into his windup, a classic high-kick, smooth-wheeling motion, straight overhand. The pitch was a hard hook that had Gun leaning away before it broke late and sneaked across the inside corner. Again Masters laughed. "You ain't seen one of them lately?"

"My machine won't do that," Gun said.

"Then you may have some trouble here."

"Shit," said the actor with the stubble.

Gun dug in deeper and waited. He expected another curve, and when the pitch came in fast, very fast and straight, he couldn't get around. Lined a foul ball into the seats off first base.

Luke's next pitch was wide of the plate, and Gun reached out and tapped it one-handed back to the pitcher's mound.

"Thanks," said Luke. Again he swung into his motion. This time Gun guessed right, a curve, and he was able to slow his stride by a whisker, time the break, and snap his wrists at the right instant. The ball whined over third base into the left-field corner.

"Hey, you're supposed to teach this guy to hit, not show off," said Luke. He was rubbing a baseball down, and trying to smile through his mustache.

Gun prepared now for the fast one. He felt the old icy lightness rising in his gut, his shoulders and arms loosening, readying themselves. And here it came, letter high, honest, nothing tricky about it. *Here's what I've got. What're you gonna do about it?*

146

# SACRIFICE

Gun's eyes, thank God, were still good and saw the ball in a kind of time warp that let him get around and put the sweet part of the bat on it. He heard the lovely sound of perfect baseball physics and watched the ball rise toward the curving glass restaurant windows in center field. It came down up there somewhere.

# 21

Gun and Diane sat together on the balcony of her room, which faced to the south. The light was gone from Lake Ontario. After the afternoon's shoot at the Skydome they'd had dinner at a Mexican place downtown—Diane had wanted Mexican beer to commemorate their evening together on her brother's boat in Florida. Then they'd strolled aimlessly through the city, covering a year's worth of ground and ending up here.

Gun found Diane as comfortable as he remembered. She didn't force a conversation in directions it didn't want to go, and Gun was so relaxed that his past rose up on its own and floated into the present. He spoke of his marriage, explained to Diane how the blindness that came from public praise had ruined him as a husband. Told her how he'd lost his wife.

"I did some reading about it," she said. Gently.

"You and everybody else."

148

Diane's strong face was kind. She was attempting to understand and likely coming close, having lived through her own share of hell. She leaned closer and her scent came to Gun on the cool lake air. "That's when you moved up to Minnesota," she said.

"And quit baseball." Gun took a sip of the coffee. Plain stuff, no flavorings, a little bitter. It was good.

"You like it up there?"

"I love it up there. It's where I belong."

"You've been by yourself for a long time."

"It's taken a long time."

"You don't get lonely?"

"Lonely is fine."

"For some people maybe." As if someone had thrown the switch on a soft lamp, the balcony suddenly grew lighter. Gun looked up and saw the moon glowing through a rip in the overcast. When Diane spoke again her voice had changed. It was quieter, tighter. "You haven't said anything about *her* yet. That makes me nervous."

"How did you know?" Gun asked.

"Give me some credit."

"I'm not sure what to say."

"Start with her name. Go from there."

"Carol Long. We've known each other for a couple years. We were planning to get married."

"Ah." Diane laughed quietly, only a little bitterness in her tone.

"We don't have to talk about this."

"Of course we do," said Diane. *"Were* planning to get married? When was this supposed to happen?"

Gun found he needed to swallow. "In a couple of days."

"A couple of days . . ." As Diane's eyes went to work on this she leaned all the way back in her chair. "You're saying what now? That you *are* getting married in a couple of days—or aren't?"

"I'm guessing that we aren't."

"Guessing?"

"Guessing, yes." Gun did his best to fill her in. He tried not to cast Carol in a bad light, but Diane didn't seem especially sympathetic.

"Sounds to me like she asked you to make an impossible choice. I'm not understanding this woman, Gun. I don't know what it is she has that you'd want."

"I won't try to explain."

"I'm glad." Diane stood and walked to the iron railing of the balcony. She had on white tights and a short black T-shirt, and looked good inside them. Gun saw her shiver, then cross her arms to warm herself.

"Come here," he told her. She sat down on his lap and he wrapped his arms around her and held her. The skin of her arms was cold and goose-bumped. The rest of her felt warm.

They sat like this long enough for Gun to realize how much he wanted her and how much he might still be wanting her years from now, if she gave him that chance. But he couldn't put Carol Long from his mind—she was here, too—and he couldn't deny that he'd spent moments with Carol as full of potential as this moment now with Diane.

"What are you thinking?" she asked.

"I wish I could say."

"That we should go inside?"

"Of course."

She stirred lightly on his lap. He felt her take a long breath and let it out carefully. His hands went to her waist, followed her contours down, and when her body trembled and pushed back against him he said, "I don't think I can let this happen, Diane."

She turned and gave Gun a look he couldn't fathom. There was disappointment in her face, but something else, too, deeper down. Gun thought of Six-Mile Point on Stony Lake and the boulders that showed themselves only in the heaviest weather, dark and shining in the troughs between breakers.

She said, "You should know something, Gun," and a muscle flexed in her jaw. "I don't like leftovers." She leaned close and kissed him once with a fervor he knew he'd remember. Then she was up and off his lap and standing above him.

He left her room and walked back to the King Edward Hotel, feeling both loss and relief, and not sure which was more appropriate.

In his room he tried calling Carol at her place but got no answer. If she'd left his parents' house this morning, she would have arrived back home in the afternoon. Early evening at the latest. Houghton, Michigan, to Stony, Minnesota, was six, seven hours by car. He tried her at the *Journal*, but no answer there, either.

He sat down on his bed to think. He could phone his parents but chose not to, imagining the discomfort of their unspoken questions coming at him through the wires. Instead he placed a call to Jack-Be-Nimble's, a tavern outside Stony. Jack LaSalle was a friend who over the years had been with Gun in some tight spots.

The phone rang half a dozen times before the gravelly voice came on. "Yeah," huffing a little. Gun pictured Jack in his white apron, phone cocked between ear and shoulder as he drew a draft beer for one of the old flannel-shirted men who claimed the bar this time of night.

"Jack, have you seen Carol?"

"She's not with you? Where are you calling from, Gun?"

"Toronto. And don't ask me why."

"Why isn't Carol up there?"

"Long story. She was driving back home today, and I'm wondering if she made it."

"Do you want me to run over to her place and have a look around?"

"No. She probably just took her time on the road. Or maybe she's having a late dinner somewhere."

"Gun, if she was gonna have a late bite, it'd be out here at my place." Jack sounded peeved. "Did you try the *Journal?*"

"Yup. Do me a favor. If she shows up tonight, give me a call. I'm at the King Edward Hotel." He gave Jack the number.

"Everything okay between the two of you?" asked Jack, ever the priest and counselor.

"We'll talk when I get back."

"Lots to talk about?"

Gun said yes and hung up. He took off his shoes and lay down on the bed, turned on the television with the remote, and started punching through channels. Talk shows, old movies, news, a ballgame. He stayed with the game, the Red Sox and Chicago, Clemens and McDowell. Turned the sound off. In fifteen minutes he was sleeping.

The knocking brought him in one motion to his feet. His brain lagged behind on the pillow, and halfway to the door he stopped to get his bearings. He asked himself what he would do if Diane Apple had reconsidered. He opened the door.

Carol Long wore a white cotton nightgown that came to just above the knee and a jean jacket over that. Tennis shoes. She wasn't smiling and her green eyes looked red and tired. Yet she seemed relaxed and warm and sure about what she was doing. He brought her into the room and sat her down on the bed. He let his eyes do the asking.

"I went home," she said. "I got there this afternoon,

about three." Carol pulled her dark hair to a knot at the back of her head and let it fall. "I took a shower and thought I'd just go to bed. I was shot. Instead I got up and drove to the Cities. Caught a flight."

"You forgot to change clothes."

Carol shrugged.

"How'd you find me?"

"Called Jack—half an hour ago from the airport here. I figured you'd be in touch with him." Carol sloughed her jean jacket from her shoulders onto the bed. The straps of her white gown were almost flourescent against her tan shoulders. She looked straight up at the ceiling and said, "Boy, oh boy."

Gun went to the phone and dialed room service and asked for a bottle of champagne. The man asked if he wanted it right away. Gun looked at Carol and changed his mind.

"Bring it up in the morning," he said.

# 22

Gun and Carol flew to Marquette after lunch and from there drove a rented car back to the Peninsula. It was after six that evening when Gun phoned Neb and Nora Summers from his parents' house. Nora took the call.

Neb, she told Gun, had checked into the hospital an hour ago. "It's happened before," she said. "The pain gets to a certain point, and it's all he can do to keep from passing out. The doctors think he'll be home in a day or two. They say he's not finished yet."

Gun expressed his regrets.

"So it's not a good time to talk to him," she said.

"It was you I wanted to see," Gun said. "If I came over, could we talk? Just the two of us?"

Nora Summers wasn't answering.

"I could come over right now."

"I don't know what we'd talk about," said Nora.

"I do," Gun said.

As he pulled up to the Summers place Nora was coming out the front door, looking around in all directions. She had on sunglasses and came quickly to Gun's window. "I'd rather we didn't talk here. Do you know that little grocery up on Stiller's Lookout?"

"I didn't know it was still going."

"It's not. Everything's all grown up around it, but the driveway still goes in. Park around back, I'll be along."

As a kid Gun had ridden his bicycle to Stiller's Lookout on nice summer days and batted rocks off the promontory, which afforded arguably the finest view of Keweenaw Bay. The little store, he remembered, was set about a quarter mile from the lake and back off the road in a stand of birch and pine. Tonight he found the driveway without difficulty and drove in slowly on the dirt trail, grasses high on both sides. The building sagging and windowless among a fresh growth of birch. He parked behind it and cut his headlights.

Ten minutes later Nora eased up in her seventies-model Mercury Monterey. Gun got out and walked up to her window. "Mosquitoes are bad, why don't I get in with you?" He went around to the passenger door and ducked into the front seat of the Mercury, amazed at the legroom. "I could get used to this kind of space," he said.

Nora was silent. The night was dark, and Gun wouldn't have been able to see her at all except she'd left her parking lights on, and the glow from the dash reached her face. She said, "I thought of telling somebody, I thought about it a lot. But who? And what could I say?" In the dim greenish light Nora's face was unhealthy.

"You can tell me," Gun said.

"I'll feel like shit."

"I bet you feel like shit already."

"And I'm afraid it's going to sound dumb. Once I say it, I mean. And I'll wish I hadn't."

"If it sounds dumb, I'll tell you it sounds dumb. Then you won't have to wonder anymore."

"I'm a loyal person, Gun. I don't turn against people. It's not in my nature to believe the worst. I'm an optimist." Her mouth came open, and her whole face started coming apart, wrinkles deepening, lines of composure blurring away. She cried, but no sound came out.

"Maybe you better just tell me."

"As long as there wasn't a body I was able to convince myself he didn't have anything to do with it. But once they found Harry . . ." Nora's jaw began trembling. "I can't turn on him like this," she said.

"You can't turn on Calvin?" Gun asked.

Nora's hands rose to her face and covered it. She spoke the name through her fingers. "Neb."

Her story left some room for interpretation, but Gun could understand why it haunted her and why she'd been unable since that night to love her husband in the same way she had before.

It had been a night of thunderstorms and heavy rain. Nora was canning pickles in her kitchen, making use of the early cucumbers from her garden. Neb was at a school board meeting. Calvin was out with friends. Nora finished up with the pressure cooker at ten and started cleaning up. By ten-thirty, the kitchen put away and dishes washed, she sat down to watch the news. Neb would be home shortly, of course, after a beer or two with his school board cronies. Calvin would be along, too. He was graduated now but still kept the curfew enforced by his father.

At ten-forty-five Calvin got in, wet from running home through the rain, and went up to bed. At eleven-thirty Nora turned off the television and called the Night Owl Bar. Neb wasn't there and hadn't been, according to Patrick Beatty, the owner and barkeep. Nora began to worry. Neb rarely stayed out late and had always been one to call.

She phoned the police desk but learned nothing. No emergencies so far tonight, and the dispatcher said she hadn't heard a thing from Neb. Was something wrong? No, said Nora. She hung up and began to ready herself for bed, her thoughts turning for the first time ever to the prospect of another woman. Was Neb unsatisfied? Was their happiness together somehow less than she imagined? She made herself a cup of hot chocolate, looked her fear straight on, and decided—with little internal struggle—that no, there could be no other woman. She and Neb had a better marriage than she'd even dared hope for.

Telling herself that her husband would soon be home with a reasonable explanation, Nora went off to bed. She even managed to sleep, despite the electrical storm and driving rain.

What woke her at two A.M. was the sucking sound of waterlogged shoes climbing the stairs. Neb's clothes were soaked through, and his face and hands were striped with mud. His eyes, Nora said, were glazed over, stunned-looking, in a way that made her wonder for an instant if he'd been struck by lightning. His movements were slow and stiff as he undressed. He was trying without success to free the stuck zipper of his trousers when Nora took his hand in her own and saw, covering his palm, the raw blisters.

Neb said they came from lifting and pushing on the rear fender of Green Tokannah's car, which had slipped into the ditch just north of town. He'd been on his way home from the meeting, he explained, when he'd seen a car off the road and stopped to help. Green was even drunker than usual, violently ill in fact, and Neb hadn't dared to leave him. So he'd helped the janitor get his car out of the ditch, then taken him back to his house, gotten him dried off and warmed up, and run some coffee into his veins. Neb had stayed with Green until the vomiting passed and then come right home. He'd simply forgotten to call, he said, and he was sorry. He seemed to mean it.

Nora wasn't satisfied. Hadn't Neb cited Green for DWI?

No, Neb told her. It was the first time he'd ever come across Green in that kind of shape while driving, and after all, the man was pathetic and didn't need another piece of bad luck. Probably too poor to pay the fine anyway.

Nora wanted to believe her husband, chose to believe him, and they went to bed. But she didn't sleep that night. For once her heart was not at peace with Neb. His story didn't feel right, and *she* didn't feel right, lying there next to him, listening to his loud, agonized breathing, seeing in her mind the glaze over his eyes, remembering how he'd avoided looking at her. And none of what he'd said made any sense to her. For one thing, Neb had never expressed anything but disdain for Green Tokannah. Sure he might've stopped to help the man out. But take him home and sober him up? Nurse him through the dry heaves for three hours, and forget to call home in the process? And not cite the man for DWI? That wasn't like Neb at all. His emotions didn't govern him when it came to his job. His reputation was for toughness and honesty.

The next morning, after Neb and Calvin had gone off to work, Nora walked to the place where Neb said that Green's car had left the road. It was a shallow ditch, recently mowed. Shallow puddles of water remained from the storm, but the lay of the ground was everywhere visible and smooth. She could find no tire tracks, no trampled grass, nothing.

Later that morning Mavis Summers had called, wondering if anyone in the family had seen her son Harry.

# 23

Gun woke the next morning to a damp breeze moving the curtains, pulled on his jeans, and walked barefoot out into a warm light rain that was blessing the tulips and glories. The grass was heavy and ankle-deep. Gunsten was on his back in the barn, oily-fingered, annoyed with the Indian.

"Listen to this idle," he said, getting up when Gun entered the barn. He straddled the bike and kicked the starter. It caught and flared, then swooned and nearly died before Gunsten saved it with some quick throttle and brought it soaring back, the hard noise banging off every flat surface in the building. Looking at Gun, the old man held up a finger, mouthed *now watch*. He released the throttle. The motor calmed to a smooth idle, coughed again, suddenly accelerated as if to burn the place down, and abruptly went out like a wind-blown match. The barn was a muted, exhaust-clouded world.

Gunsten said, amidst fumes and silence, "Nuts."

"It sounds good while you're goosing it."

"So I'm fine, long as I drive real fast."

"That should suit you. Carburetor?"

Gunsten twisted his neck, spoke sorely: "I've had it apart, it's clean. Fuel line's good. You know," he said, lifting his brows, "even with all these years, and this motorbike, and the Hacker out to the lake, I've never really been at peace with machines. Engines, I mean."

Gun felt a little stunned by this admission. What had his father ever failed to fix?

"Oh, I can work on 'em, sure. But it's not what I favor."

"I don't remember the bike ever needing much work," Gun said.

"It's been a faithful one. I owe it a headache or two." Gunsten went to one of the age-blackened eight-by-eights that supported the haymow joists and plucked a cotton rag off a nail. He worked the oil from his hands slowly, the tendons rising in his forearms. His eyes gave nothing away when he looked back to Gun. "So. Did you learn things out in Toronto?"

"I learned you're well in the clear."

"Hmm. That would dim someone else's prospects, wouldn't it?" Gunsten's voice was tired, like an old thought that just won't rest.

"Do you know who, Dad?"

Silence in the barn, and blue smoke drifting.

"Dad. We ought to talk to him. I'll understand if you don't want to, but he owes us the truth. He owes *you.*"

Gunsten rehung the rag with a worn-out gesture, his wide shoulders hooking forward under his shirt. He said, "While you were gone, son, Neb Summers took a bad turn."

"I know. He's in the hospital. Nora told me how it hits him sometimes."

"Well, it hit him worse this time. I called this morning, say hello. Doctor said he had a stroke. He was lying in bed, and the nurse took in his breakfast. And he wouldn't wake up."

*Not now,* Gun thought.

Gunsten walked heavily to the motorcycle and sat. "A light stroke is what the doctor said. He can talk and understand, but he's weak."

"He was weak before," Gun said, trying to digest this. It didn't make anything easier. What now? Stay quiet? Did you acquit a dying man of murder and call his disease his punishment? "How much time does he have?"

"Depends. He could recover from the stroke, but the cancer likely won't give him time."

Gun hated saying it. "Neb killed Harry, Dad. He came in late that night. Nora saw him taking off his clothes. They were muddy from the grave."

His father said nothing, but his face showed old wires suddenly connecting, giving him current.

"Does this make sense to you?"

"Well, let me see. I recall wondering, years ago . . . Gun, was Nora sure? Did Neb ever tell her anything?"

"Never a word. It was clear enough." He told Gunsten about Nora Summers's fears, about Neb's unlikely charity toward Green Tokannah, about the great uncle's hunch that Harry'd been about to hop the border.

"Well." Gunsten seemed chagrined—not particularly sorrowful anymore, but angry with himself. "It seems like I'm to blame after all, in a way."

Gun had nothing to say. He waited, and finally his father tilted a look at him that was as curious and open as any he'd ever seen.

"Son," Gunsten said, "you want to know the real reason young Harry had those keys?"

162

# 24

*H*arry Summers came to me saying he wanted a job. And I suppose he did, though when I think about it, it was a friend he wanted. More than a friend. A savior."

They'd gone into the house, where Madilyn had wordlessly set about brewing coffee. Gunsten headed her off, though, asked her to sit, and pulled out a chair for her. He took her hand and held it in his as he continued.

"It wasn't long after the day you and he first went up to the park and hit the ball around. I suppose he felt more comfortable here after that. He wanted to help me part-time, learn some carpentering. Turned out he was a good worker, no surprise. And a good talker—a kid still in high school, you don't expect they're thinking about much except cars and sports and looking good when the girls walk by. Did you know his folks held him back? He was nineteen when he graduated."

"Bad age to be in nineteen sixty-nine."

His father nodded. "We didn't have many going to Vietnam from Copper Strike. It was getting to be an old folks' town even then. But there was the Blocker kid—remember?—who got crushed by the helicopter outside of Saigon. And Jerry Essola, only a year older than Harry. They grew up on the same block. Anyhow, I let Harry come do some work for me, and pretty soon he let me hear what direction he was thinking."

"North would be my guess."

"He had that great uncle in Toronto, the one you went to visit." Gunsten foresaw the question and shook his head. "Naw, Harry never told him he was coming. Didn't want any relations getting in trouble over him. But son, he wanted out of this country like I've never seen a boy want anything."

Madilyn said, "Could you blame him for that? It wasn't like he had roots here. His people were in Canada."

"I didn't blame him, Madilyn. I agreed with him. You know about Neb Summers, moving from Quebec so as to get citizenship. He wasn't here six months before his younger brother followed, and they both went happily off to Korea. Duty-loving men, and I don't fault them for it. But when Vietnam got rolling Neb prodded his boy Calvin into enlisting and thought Harry should do the same."

"But Myron, Harry's dad," Gun said. "He didn't buy that, did he?"

"Myron saw a lot of action in Korea, more than Neb did. He came home and watched his kid grow up and somewhere along the way decided war wasn't the greatest thing that could happen to a man after all. I don't think he counseled Harry to head for Canada, but he wouldn't have discouraged it.

"Then one morning, lovely day, we were roofing the

new addition on Curtis Fording's place. You know. It was cool, and we were sitting on the roof waiting for the sun to warm up the tarpaper so it wouldn't crack when we rolled it out, and Harry looked at me and said he'd gotten notice. He had his draft card with him. Wanted to know what he should do."

Madilyn pulled her hand away and crossed her arms. Carol ghosted in wearing a hunter-green robe, her eyes full of listening, and took a chair.

"I asked him where his allegiance was. He was quiet about it for a few days. We finished Curtis's roof. Sometime after that Harry asked me for help. He knew I had the boat. He wanted me to take him across the lake late at night, drop him at the Canadian shore. I said I'd do it."

Gun shook his head. "Dad, why didn't he just drive across? I knew guys who did that—they showed their draft cards, told Customs they were going for a weekend, and never came back. Nothing to it."

"If he'd thought of that before he burned his draft card, maybe he'd still be alive."

"He burned his card?" Carol asked. "There were protests in Copper Strike?"

"He didn't do it to protest. Told me he was afraid he wouldn't go through with his decision unless he locked himself into it. So he burned it, out back in his mama's garden—and then realized how hard the world had suddenly become."

"Would they have checked for the card at Customs?"

Gunsten nodded. "Pretty much always. If a kid had been notified and couldn't show his card at the border, it was trouble. So we agreed on a night. I gave him the keys and told him to get there early, I'd be out later. And he never got there."

Outside it was darker, the warm rain coming hard enough now to be a dull drumming against the house.

Madilyn got up and turned on the light over the sink. She started coffee and took four coffee cups from the cabinet. In the part of Gun's mind that was not preoccupied he thought. Hasn't he told her these things? His wife? And she isn't asking why not. At least she wasn't now, in front of Gun and Carol.

"And you never mentioned any of this to Myron or Neb after Harry went missing. How come, Dad?"

"Because it didn't mean anything. I knew about him burning the card, but when he didn't show up that night it left me as much in the dark as anyone else. Popular theory was he'd gone to Canada. And he had, for all I knew. I wasn't the only fellow around with a boat."

Gun gave his father a long look. Gunsten returned it without a flinch and said finally: "You tell me how it would've helped, then, going to Myron. Going to Neb."

But Gun couldn't. Harry Summers had had his skull crushed with a hammer one night in a rainstorm. It wasn't a thing that could be fixed by a retroactive conscience. Not even his father's.

He sighed and accepted a cup of coffee from Madilyn. What was she thinking, this brisk woman, hearing all this for the first time? But she said nothing, just poured her husband coffee and set it down in front of him, brushing his lined cheek with the tips of her fingers as she moved away.

"I still think we have to talk to Neb," Gun said. They had pulled back from conversation and resided for a time in silence, listening to the rain, occasionally refilling their cups. The house smelled of dampness and hot chicoried coffee and lingering oil from Gunsten's fingers where he'd wiped them with the rag.

"Let's give him another day. The man's had a stroke, it's not a good time for confrontation."

166

"Then I'll go see Calvin. It's funny—he was pretty straight with me the night of the funeral. I didn't expect it. He was ripped about the whole thing, of course, but honest, too."

"I'll go with you," Carol said.

"Not this time. What if he wants to dance?"

Carol didn't press.

Gunsten said, "You think he knows it might've been his own old man who killed his favorite cousin?"

"Can't hurt to ask."

"I disagree. Calvin has large reactions." His father gave a cautionary smile.

He got up to go. His stomach felt heavy and dissatisfied from the coffee. That chicory—odd stuff. He took his canvas jacket off the hook by the door and slung it on as he went out. The rain was beating itself into mist on the gravel driveway, and he stood on the porch to watch it a minute. Behind him Carol said, speaking through the screen door, "Be careful, Gun."

She looked so good.

"Ever and always," he said.

# 25

Calvin Summers had left Copper Strike twice that Gun knew of: once in the fall of '69 for Vietnam, where he'd served a couple of tours and earned the Silver Star, and again in 1980 when a lightning fire took the one-story prefab he'd set up on a small jackpine acreage near town. The incident was local legend. He'd been drinking at Speed's the night of the fire when lightning doused the electricity. It was nigh on to closing, so Calvin and the woman who was living with him then left for home. They were driving a Buick from which the back window had been broken years earlier, which was bad for Cal but fine for the woman's assortment of cats, which slept in there on rainy nights. They drove through the wind and darkness, anyhow, and soon saw the flames, atop the pines, chewing an orange hole out of the night. Calvin never talked of it, but the woman did, for years thereafter, and she said they never even sped up. She said they drove slowly on toward home, knowing where the fire was and where it was headed, and that Calvin reached into the back seat twice on the way for beers. Michelobs. She said they turned into the weedy drive just as the flames turned the walls of the prefab to a black transparency, like a Kodak negative viewed against the light, and only then did Calvin stop. He told her to get out of the car. The house trembled like a mirage. Calvin reached back once more to get the last Mick, then slipped the automatic into drive and stepped out. The Buick rolled forward, moving easily and gaining speed. It hit the house just to the left of the front door. The woman said it went through the wall like a hippo hitting a nylon tent; just went on through and disappeared, and the shock brought the whole mess down. Calvin opened the Michelob and handed it to her; told her, so went the legend, "A car like that, I'd rather start over again with nothing."

Now Calvin lived alone on one of the back residential streets. It was a skinny two-story place with gray asphalt siding and a despairing tilt that said something about the sort of luck he'd had starting over in Detroit. Gun parked on the street. It was still raining. Calvin's neighborhood smelled like bad drains and old sausage.

"Calvin?" Nobody answered his knock, but the door was unlocked. "Cal?"

The house looked unlucky inside, too. Old candy-stripe carpet, cigarette-stained. Old Magnavox coffin-sized console TV. Orange vinyl couch like from a cut-rate dentist's waiting room.

"Back here, Pedersen." Calvin's voice drifted in from the backyard. "Door's off the kitchen, come on out." Gun groped his way through a glut of heaped laundry baskets, boxes of foul milk cartons and *Penthouse* magazines. What kitchen? Ah—there, the back door.

"Gun, you shifty son of a bitch." Calvin was at the rear of his property under a clear plastic lean-to at the side of his garage. He had a white apron on and a wheelbarrow full of wet cement beside him under the lean-to. He was sitting on a stack of bricks. He was grinning.

"Got enough room under there?" It was no typhoon, but a good plentiful rain.

"Sure. Come on, get dry." Cal shifted on the bricks and hoisted up a bucket full of ice cubes and longnecks. "Well, not *dry,* exactly."

Even in the backyard Gun had to walk carefully. There were pieces of automobiles, an airplane propeller, a defunct record player amongst the grass and milkweed. Calvin clearly didn't waste money on landfill fees.

"I stopped by your realty office. Nobody there."

"Yeah, business sucks on rainy days. How I love being self-employed. Have a beer."

"Thanks." Gun accepted a bottle. He left the cap on. "We need to talk a little, Cal."

"Yes, we do. We do at that." On the ground, next to a square spaded hole in the turf, six longnecks were already empty. "You like my handiwork here?"

"You're building a barbecue."

"A nice wide pit, that's the secret. You don't want to crowd the coals. I'm using brick, see? Add some value to the property."

"I was sorry to hear about your dad, Cal. How's he doing?"

"That's a good look, Pedersen, with the concerned eyes and all. I almost think you care. I'd buy it for sure if I didn't know how much you wanna bury him."

Uh-oh, Gun thought. "I just want to talk, Calvin."

"Talk away. You went to Uncle Max's, right? How is the old coot?" Calvin picked up a pointed trowel and jabbed at the wet cement.

170

"Seems all there." Gun paused. Inches above his head the rain tapped soggily on the plastic tarp. "Cal, did Harry ever think about skipping the draft? With Canada so close."

"A Summers pass up a war? Max must've told you that's an unlikely prospect. We ain't that smart in this family, Pedersen."

"I talked to your mom, too."

Calvin snorted through a nose that sounded full. "That's very swell. You go see Max, and then my ma. Two of Dad's biggest fans. You know, me and her don't have much to say since she got out of stir."

Gun didn't answer.

"What, that's something you didn't know? She's nuts, Gun-o. A mental case, got a file two inches thick."

"I'm glad you're there for her, Calvin."

"Did you know she tried to leave my dad? I was in Nam then. She just checked out. Packed a cardboard box up with clothes—Dad wrote me about it. He found her trying to start the Olds. She had a bobby pin in her hand, thought it was the car key." Calvin troweled up mud and slapped some on a brick. "She tell you some interesting stuff?"

"She told me Neb killed Harry."

"Well, she's mighty credible, Gun-o. Did I tell you about the shock therapy? Three treatments, that's all it took. Wham! That blew the clouds away. A little electrode happiness. Welcome back, Ma, here's your brain in a little blue box, talk softly now and don't get it excited." The trowel moved around like a machete in the wet cement. Gun guessed it was six, seven feet between him and Calvin, and the big guy didn't look quick on his feet today. Safe enough.

He said, "She was convincing about it, Calvin. I'm sorry about the timing."

"Yeah, I can see how sorry you are. You know, I had

it wrong. You're still just deflecting the blame. Don't want your old man to take the heat." Calvin's little eyes went pouty in his round, bland face, and it struck Gun that nothing changed; they were two boys on a playground, arguing about their fathers.

"Calvin, I'm going now. I'm sorry about Neb, and about your mom."

Calvin dropped the trowel and reached for a beer. He twisted the cap off. He wouldn't look at Gun.

"But I have to ask, Cal. Did you know that your dad killed Harry?"

Calvin tilted up a swallow, took his time letting it go down. His voice was calm. "I don't believe this. Pedersen, don't you know my old man at all?"

"Has he ever had difficulty with money? Ever asked you for any?"

Calvin stared at him in disbelief. "What if he did? Look around. You think I could help him much? You're dumb as a damn brick, Gun-o." He lurched to his feet suddenly, picked a brick off the pile, and lobbed it. "Catch."

Gun caught it, dropping the beer bottle which broke hitting the ground. Calvin smiled, a recess bully. He grabbed another brick and tossed it. No lob this time. It bounced off Gun's chest and surprised a cough from his lungs.

"Whoops! Come on, ballplayer, get the glove up," Calvin said, and the third brick sailed over Gun's shoulder while Gun moved in, got Calvin under the armpits, and lifted. It was all instinct and no thought, and Gun felt his back compress and shudder with Calvin's two hundred twisting pounds, and then Calvin's head went through the plastic tarp above and a pool of cold rainwater broke in on them, and Gun let go. Calvin landed *schlupp* on his butt in the wheelbar-row, wet cement splashing over the sides and pooling in his lap. He looked down at himself and then at Gun, his eyebrows halfway up his forehead.

"Holy—" he said, then he hiccuped and started to laugh.

"Yup," Gun said, hiding a gasp. His lower back was cramping, the muscles grouping around to protect his poor shocked spine.

Calvin laughed harder, howling in his wheelbarrow while the rain dripped down from the hole in the tarp and made milky puddles in the cement. "Hoo hoo, Pedersen. Hoo hoo! Hand me a brew, hey? Hee!"

Gun bent tenderly down and hooked a longneck between two fingers. He said, "Here, Cal-o," which set Calvin's noise up another notch, then picked his way through the yard and around the house, moving like a guy he'd known once in a therapy ward who'd been struck on the hip by a milk truck.

Calvin was still braying when Gun got to the Dodge.

If the pain in his back hadn't been so insistent, he probably would have paid more attention to the rearview mirror as he pulled away from the curb. He did glimpse a vehicle slowing down in front of Calvin's house; later he would wonder what he might have noticed, had he been in a noticing mood. But the pain was enormous, and he took his eyes from the mirror and so missed details: the shiny grille, the slow reconnaissance pace, the neon-green paint in a town as gray as a prison in a Merle Haggard song.

# 26

*H*e stopped at Hayes Drug before leaving town and bought a jar of Advil. He dry-swallowed. He'd endured back spasms before, and you had to handle them right away; otherwise they turned into Simon Legree, owning your life and making it hurt.

His parents were gone when he arrived. So was Carol. He creaked up the porch steps, his backbone feeling like a column of blocks stacked off-center, and went into the guest bedroom. He went to one knee and pulled a pillow out from under the spread, dropped the pillow next to the bed and laid himself out on the planked pine floor, his back at last beginning to relax with the pressure and support of the wood. He took a breath, his first deep one since lifting Calvin. What a brilliant strategem. Someday he'd remember he was closing in on fifty.

He lay there like that, listening to the sounds of the empty house, until the Advil started to traffic through his bloodstream. This sort of thing had happened a few times back with the Tigers, including once down the stretch drive in 1968 when he'd slipped chasing down a gapper in the rain. He'd been locked up tight for two days, damning all doctors. The team trainer had explained how the back muscles overlapped, like scallops, and the wrong motion triggered a domino freeze-up until you were stiff as a dead armadillo. There was nothing for it but to relax. Gun breathed shallowly in the darkened room until the floor began to rotate, and the medicine moved through his veins with an almost audible shuffle, like sawdust sliding through plastic straws.

He slept without dreams for once, waking after three hours with the sensation that he'd been wrapped tightly in foil: in darkness, unable to move, a taste like nickel on his tongue. His back ached, but only slightly. Cautiously he rolled to his left and sat up.

No bad twinges.

So the worst of it was gone, and so was the doubt Gun had been feeling about what to do next. Maybe Nora Summers was exactly what Calvin said she was; maybe she'd invented the story against Neb because she needed it somehow to comfort her damaged psyche. But there was one more person who might shine a beam back into that rainy night when Harry died, and that was Green, the drunken janitor who'd ostensibly driven into the muddy ditch only minutes before Neb Summers happened along.

Gun got to his feet. His back handled the trip to the kitchen without jitters. The house was still empty.

He took three eggs from the refrigerator, thick-shelled brown eggs Madilyn bought from Sally Hedley down the road, and stirred them up in a crockery bowl with a wire whisk. He laid a copper pan on the stove, poured in oil, and set the flame to tickle the copper.

There was one big mushroom left in a plastic carton, and also the venison sausage. No onions; but a handful of fresh chives had sprung up among the tulips, and he chopped them fine and threw them in the hot oil.

He had an idea about Green, but it needed to simmer a little. He chopped the mushroom, cubed the sausage, and wished for cheese.

The old janitor, he suspected, would rather not talk about that night. Maybe he *had* gone into the ditch and been rescued by Neb Summers. Maybe not. For twenty-five years it hadn't mattered. Maybe now it did.

He ground pepper onto the omelet, flipped it over, and turned off the heat before he thought of toast. An essential. He probed the proper cabinet and was grateful; Madilyn, God bless and reward her, still baked her own bread.

He thought he had it now, the way to approach Green. It would take some care. A set of ethics could rust a lot in twenty-five years, and working the truth from such frozen gears could take a lot of pulling.

The Sidewalks Tavern was a square blue clapboard place next to the highway a few miles south of Copper Strike. It didn't have a sidewalk anymore, but once it had, and the sidewalk had led to a short street full of commerce: a dry cleaner, a mercantile, and a white church with a steeple. There had been homes and a wooden schoolhouse and a proud sign telling the community's name, Roofing. Now everything except the Sidewalks was gone, rotted to dust. The tavern still stood, smelly and victorious. Like most of its patrons, it was a tough little bastard.

Green Tokannah was on the third stool from the end when Gun walked in. It was a quarter past six, and the bar smelled of booze and frying fat. Green had on his work khakis. His large square hands were bunched on the bar, protecting a shot glass. There was music from an ugly aluminum juke, the Rolling Stones.

Gun took the neighboring stool. The music was a little too loud, and he hoped the old janitor would enunciate. "Evening, Green."

Green gave a low, preoccupied bark.

"Excuse me?"

"Armp!" Green said. A dime's worth of something rolled around in the bottom of the shot glass.

"Ah," Gun said.

The bartender was a pulpy, satisfied-looking man in middle age who'd committed a bad shave that morning. His cheeks were full of gooseflesh with the tips nipped off. "You with the Green Man today?"

Gun nodded.

"I'll buy you a drink, then."

"A beer."

"Friend of the Green Man, friend of mine," the bartender said. "Green's our local color."

The janitor contributed nothing to this. The bartender drew a beer, glancing at Gun, then smiled as he beheaded the brew and filled the glass high. He brought it and leaned over the bar. "Tigers ain't the same without you. Shameful. All those homers and no average at all."

"Nor any pitching. You have a kind memory."

"Accurate."

"I'd like to buy Green a drink." That got the old guy's attention, Green's big blood-vesseled face coming around full of want and suspicion.

"You want what from me?" the janitor demanded.

"Talk."

"Huh. You don't want that. I talk funny." He said it

177

with such bitter honesty that Gun hurt for the darkness of the old man's years; decades spent on a stool in this syrupy tavern. Smelling this smell. Life in the crease.

Green looked at the bartender. "Bourbon, then, if he wants to buy it."

Gun said nothing while the bartender fetched the bottle and poured Green a shot. Green took it in three slow hits and laid the glass on the bar. He turned to Gun, caught his eye but couldn't hold it. Settled for his chin. "Stomach's all to hell these days. Thanks for the drink."

"You're welcome."

"I don't much like talking." The janitor's speech was guttural but seemed improved. He had, Gun supposed, the home-field advantage.

Another customer came in, a middle-aged woman wearing tight black pants and a jean jacket with a black POW patch on the sleeve. Gun waited for the bartender to move down and greet her before saying, "You want to tell me about the night Harry was killed?"

Green picked up the shot glass and turned it over. Not a drop fell out. "No. No, sir."

"The night you drove into the ditch," Gun said. "Neb Summers came along, gave you a push to get out."

"Nope."

"Nope, he didn't push you out?"

"Nope, I'm not talkin'. It's too old. I forget now."

Down the bar the woman was having supper: a tequila sunrise, glass of beer, a paper tray full of onion rings. The jukebox was playing an old Bonnie Raitt song, her tired, sweet voice just aching for a man to trust.

"Neb's been a decent friend to you, Green?"

178

The janitor nodded slightly. Or it could have been the bourbon.

"Also to me, and to my folks. I'm not trying to hang him."

Green straightened. He swiveled toward Gun. There was matter crusted at the corners of his eyes. "Hell you ain't. Now listen. Two things: Neb's a bastard. Okay? Not a killer, a bastard. *Armp!* And he's carried me. Forty years he carried me."

"I don't follow."

"You don't need to." Green undid the black button of his shirt pocket and jabbed around inside it, coming out with a few crumpled bills. He dropped them beside the shot glass and slid off his stool.

Gun watched him swing steadily along the dark wood floor, same gait as he'd always used in schooltime hours, lacking only a broom. He hesitated a moment at the door, as if preparing himself for the light, and went out. Gun rose and beckoned the bartender.

He caught up with Green in the parking lot. The janitor was standing by a black topless Willys Jeep that looked made of earth and rust. It was next to Gun's rented car.

"Green, let's take a ride."

"Nothin' to say."

"You don't have to talk. Let's go."

Green replied with a stream of grunts that defied interpretation and made Gun despise what he was doing: forcing the old man from his last place of comfort, forcing meaning from his speech. Green's fingers shook on the door handle of the Jeep, and Gun decided to play one more despicable card. He pulled from his pocket the bottle of decent bourbon he'd bought from the bartender and held it up for Green to see.

"Huh. You think that's all I need?"

"No." *I think you need to tell the truth,* Gun said silently. *I think you need to remember.*

"I don't need it."

"I didn't intend to insult you," Gun said. He pocketed the bottle.

Green stuck a key in the ignition but didn't turn it. "You were scared o' me back then," he said.

Gun heard pride in the claim. "I was terrified. I thought you might be the devil."

The janitor frowned, and for an instant Gun discerned a remnant of the old menace that had owned a knuckly grip on the imaginations of a thousand children. The devil grunted and held out his hand for the bourbon.

"My car," Gun said.

# 27

They drove toward Copper Strike with the sun setting through the pines and hardwoods on their left. Green made himself at home in the Dodge, knees propped against the dash, arms resting on his thighs, the bottle open in his shirt pocket. He wasn't hurrying with the bourbon but plainly enjoyed its presence.

"You said Neb carried you. I don't understand," Gun said. They didn't have far to go, and he wanted Green to talk a little before their destination become too clear.

"Way the hell back. There were a bunch of kids, *armp!* got in the building one night. Broke into supply. My shift. Took a fire 'stinguisher, brooms, buckets. Anything they could smash with."

"Yeah." Gun couldn't remember the incident, only the story. It was part of Green's legend, what he'd done to those kids.

"They started one end of the main hall. Biology room, the big fish tank. Smashed it all to hell. Glass, cabinets, a whole room. They were gonna do the whole school."

Gun waited. He knew what had happened, everyone did; Green had sneaked into the room and doused the lights. The vandals—there were five—went panicky, and as they scrambled in the darkness Green stepped into their midst with a broom handle and gave them the worst of his inarticulate rage. The unseen thrashing must have seemed to those kids like the whipping tail of Satan. They fled screaming, and when their bruises revealed them, days later, to be the sons of local disreputables, and not those of town or school officials, Green was clapped on the back and given a raise.

"And I didn't do nothin'," Green said. He took a quick snap from the bottle and gave Gun a challenging glare. "Too drunk. I had whiskey, down the boiler room. Asleep on my arse."

"You mean you didn't whack those kids?"

"Neb was going by. He was a strong bastard then."

Neb? "I don't get it."

Green looked at him like he was back in third grade. "He was driving by. Mr. Cop. Saw the lights on, junk flying around. He always had a key, so he came in. Musta been fun, out the lights, swing that stick a little." The janitor paused. "He woke me up after. Found me at the boiler and screamed good. I'd'a lost my job."

"Except he never told. He let you take the credit."

Green was quiet as they passed into Copper Strike. The sun lay behind the edge of the west, nothing left but a marigold glow that ascended into deep blue. Stars were beginning in the east in the dark wash of sky over Superior.

At last the old man capped the bottle. "I had to have

182

work. I ast him not to say. Cried, a damn drunk little baby. What else could I'a' done? Well. He felt sorry for ol' Green."

"You weren't so old then."

Green didn't answer.

"So you figured you owed Neb Summers. Owed him quite a bit."

"Armp."

Gun pulled into the back lot of the quilted-looking police station. There were only two cars there: the city's round-edged Taurus with the cherry on top, and an LTD old enough to have square corners. Henry Littenen's car.

"Uh-uh," Green said.

"Come on."

The janitor didn't resist, which was just as well.

Harry Summers's bones still rested in the haphazard order James Work had left them in. They lay on a folded cotton sheet in a long metal drawer in a windowless basement room. The walls were painted a shade of dark yellow Gun guessed would seem familiar to drunks and sheep farmers.

"Okay," Henry Littenen said. He was standing next to the open drawer with his arms crossed and his little Panasonic tape recorder on top of the metal cabinet. Green was facing away. Gun was looking at the bones because he couldn't help trying to connect them, somehow, with the shy grinning kid he'd hit baseballs to in the autumn of '68. The kid with the good pick and the promising arm.

The bones, as Madilyn had said, were almost black.

"Okay," Henry repeated. He pressed a button on the recorder. "Green Tokannah, twenty-seven May nineteen ninety-three. Green, I have to ask you what you know about Harry Summers's death."

Green wouldn't speak.

Henry looked at Gun and continued. "Green. It's not easy for any of us."

"Go to hell."

"Near as we know, Green, Harry was seen alive on June twelve of nineteen sixty-nine. That night there was a bad storm. A lot of rain. You remember it?"

No answer.

"I wish you'd look at me, Green."

"Stop saying my name."

On the cotton sheet Harry's skull lay on its side, a charcoal dome. There were some teeth around it, loose. An L-shaped crack started over the left eye socket and turned upward. A hard dry sadness blocked Gun's throat.

"You remember the storm?"

Green nodded.

"Were you out in it?"

"Yuh."

"Green—I'm sorry—were you out driving in that rain?"

"I drove."

"Did you go into the ditch? The visibility would've been terrible. Slippery roads." Henry seemed to be leading Green, but by now Gun didn't care. The bones, Henry's dry voice droning, the close yellow-painted walls; the room itself was a box full of age and mortality. You couldn't stand in here and imagine youth. The air was like bad cabbage in your nostrils.

"Come on, Green," Henry said.

"Let me be."

A drop of sweat curled down from Gun's brow, and he pressed his eyes shut. He tried to put himself back on that October ballfield, a wind at his back and a bat in his hands, smacking grounders and line drives to a young man who couldn't have known his future was almost spent. But the picture wouldn't complete itself. In his imagination every swing he took was painful, full of stiffness and arthritic grief, and the balls rolled slowly across the diamond, dying in the grass. And Harry, out there at shortstop, he was all wrong, too—not quick and limber but a crooked figure who took the small cautious steps of an old man. Gun's memory panicked, tried to supply young Harry's countenance and failed; two stagnant eyes in a papyrus face stared at him across the ballyard.

"Green," Henry Littenen said, "Neb Summers says he helped you out that night. Pushed your car out of the ditch and took you home. Stayed at your place a while. You can tell me yes or no."

Gun opened his eyes, saw the set of Green's shoulders, and knew he wasn't going to talk.

Henry was getting nervous with the silence. "It'll come down to a subpoena for sure, Green. You rather have to say it all in court?"

Gun put his hand out to the long spread of bones. He chose an upper leg, a femur, because he was standing a ways from Green and needed the reach. He wished comfort upon Harry's soul. He picked up the bone. It was light and sandy-textured against his fingers.

Green, his back to them still, was grunting "Waste of time" when Gun laid Harry's femur across his cheek. The old janitor spun at the touch. "Goddamn! *Armp!* You're nuts, Pedersen!" He scuttled backward away from the bone, but still Gun kept it aimed, a divining rod.

"Remember, Green," Gun said.

Henry started to talk but stopped himself. Gun stepped around the drawer and put the bone under the old man's nose. Green retreated again, scuffing backward in his thick black shoes with his mouth open and his wet tongue clicking but producing no words. Gun stayed with him, pointing. Another step and Green ran out of floor, bumped against the wall and stayed as if pinned, nailed to the dark yellow wall beneath a big slow black-handed clock.

They stayed that way while the second hand crept through a standstill minute, Green with his pink-rimmed eyes thinking hard and the bone touching the pouchy flesh under his chin, Gun fresh out of pity for this pitiful man and needful of audible truth.

"Wasn't any ditch," Green said.

Henry moved the tape recorder closer.

"I got off work. Locked up. Rainy as hell when I went out to the car. I backed out, and the headlights came around and showed somebody over at the field. Headlights showed 'em back of that dugout there."

Gun lowered Harry's femur an inch.

"Couldn't see who. Goddamn high schoolers, always playing at something . . . I shut off the car and went down. In the rain that way." Green's eyes widened, and he sneezed without warning, as if the memory resided in his sinuses. "He was waist deep, digging. Neb Summers. He didn't yell at me. I thought he would."

Henry asked, "Did you see Harry?"

"'Course I did. Worst thing I ever saw, him on the ground and that hammer stickin' outa his mouth. Neb diggin' the grave." Green's voice was soft, clearer than usual. "He'd been bawlin', the bastard, eyes all red."

"Did he say why he did it?"

"Said the boy was gonna run from the war. Told me that later."

186

Gun said, "Green? Do you know why he left the hammer that way?"

"Couldn't get it out the boy's mouth. He bent over and pulled once—Neb was moanin'—but it was wedged. Looked like Harry wouldn't let go. Like a dog with a deer shank."

The picture took some time to sink in and fade. Finally Henry said, his voice thin, "You never said a thing."

"Who'm I gonna tell? Neb's the police. People know him. He told me how it'd look." Green stopped abruptly, gave a soft *armp* of embarrassment and sorrow. "Said it looked to him like *I* killed the kid—maybe he was dinkin' around the school. Like with those others. Like I was drunk, got wild."

"What others?" said Henry.

Green didn't answer but looked at Gun, who said, "They busted up a classroom. You remember. Green supposedly cut the lights and went in swinging." He looked closely at the janitor, the flame of botched capillaries, and pity returned. If Green wanted everyone to know his fabled defense of property was a fraud, he could tell them himself.

Henry said, "Oh, yeah."

Gun stepped back and re-placed the bone with the rest of Harry.

"What was I s'posed to do?" Green said.

Gun said, "You finished, Henry? I'll drive him home."

Henry nodded blankly. A telephone buzzed, and he picked it up and turned his back.

"I pertected myself," Green said.

As they left the bones and the yellow-painted room, walking in silence through fluorescent halls and dim stairwells and finally out to the free dark air, still silent, a window slid open in Gun's imagination and he saw without struggle the young glad shape of Harry Summers, his blond hair straightened back by wind, eyes given in concentration, running across a bright green diamond toward something almost within his reach.

# 28

Green muttered some on the ride home but said nothing that urged a reply, and Gun let him out in front of a tarpapered house with a ripped plastic snow fence encircling the yard. The porch light was on and Gun watched the old janitor stump up and push open the unlocked door. It wasn't more than four inches ajar when a brown-striped bolt of cat tore through it like a soul fleeing torment, but Green was prepared and snagged the cat by its loose nape and carried it into the house. A light went on and the door closed.

Gun rolled down every window in the car and pulled away. There were smells that he wanted gone: bourbon, bad tobacco, the rotten sadness of an old man with not much left or much attempted. He drove slowly, the wind entering in silver sheets around his shoulders and the moon giving him such a clear road he could've done without headlights. Then the Dodge

topped a short rise and he saw, away to his left on a
township road he'd not driven in decades, the flashing
cherry atop Henry Littenen's police car. It shone red
on the road, on standing water in the steep ditch, and
on the rising chrome bumper of a pickup truck that
lay on its side in the weeds.

The truck was bright green. Henry was down at
water's edge, pointing a long black flashlight at something in the ditch and talking into a hand-held radio.
Gun stood from the car but stayed well back; no
suspense here. The cherry blinked away, the truck's
vertical bug shield reading, bottom to top, ANY
TIME ANY PLACE.

"You know him?" Gun called.

"Name's Dandrie," Henry answered. He stepped
away, keeping the beam on the water. Dandrie lay in
the ditch with his clothes mucked a salamander
brown, his hair twisted and flattened, his arms adrift.
The water wasn't more than a foot deep where he
was.

"Drunk for sure," Henry said. "I can smell him
from here. Look at the truck, how the door's open—
he drove into the ditch, crawled outa the cab, was too
stinking to walk away."

"He's dead?"

"His mouth's underwater." Henry was wearing his
trooper hat, and now he slid it down to cover his face
and spoke through it. "Pedersen, this day's been a
crapper."

"Yeah. Ambulance coming?"

"I called Jarvey before coming out. He's got EMT
duty tonight." Henry replaced the hat. "Sometimes
Jarvey has trouble with engines."

Gun supposed there was no rush. "Who called it
in?"

"Lisa took the call. Somebody saw it from the
highway, didn't know how long it'd been here or if

anyone was hurt. Most people, you know, they just keep on driving."

At home he declined a reheated supper, regretting it because Madilyn's venison roast was worthy of attention, but Dandrie floated uneasily on his mind and deprived him of appetite. He'd meant to learn more about Dandrie, like who he was, and why he'd chewed out Calvin Summers in open view that night at Speed Ruona's. It struck Gun that Cal wasn't the type to endure public floggings, and there was something else, a half memory. Hadn't he seen Dandrie's truck, or one like it, cruising Calvin's street? He poked at that one for a while but it wouldn't squeal, and besides there was more important news to give Carol and his parents. He described Green's story of witnessing Neb at the ballpark. It was tough telling it.

"I think," Gunsten said when he was finished, "I'll go see Neb in the morning."

Gun stretched his arms, joints in both shoulders popping in relief. "In the morning I'm taking a long walk. I've had enough of confessions for a while."

Gunsten had left for the hospital after breakfast, and Carol walked with Gun, which was what he'd hoped for: Carol quiet and tramping delicately in pointy tanned-leather boots while the sun got up and stood at a distance. They were walking beside the narrow stream that still flowed with the melt from snows higher up, and she looked like something that had sprung up next to it and grown there, her jeans of green canvas, the jacket she'd made from a red-brown Chief Joseph blanket. A soft blanket, but his hand on her waist knew the easy strength beneath.

"What will Neb say to Gunsten?" she asked at last.

They walked on while he thought it over. "He could die tomorrow."

"Does that make a person more truthful?"

"I hope so."

The stream jumped along through an area where the earth was soft and lumpy and full of tall grasses and sparse willow. Song sparrows trilled from invisible perches, the songs going quiet when their steps came too close, then opening up wide and jubilant again behind them; once a grouse broke from hiding with a noise like a startled two-fisted heart, and Gun saw Carol freeze and sight the bird, a misty perspiration on her upper lip.

"Want to turn back?" he asked.

"A little further."

Near the back edge of Pedersen property the land rose and the stream pooled and fell off to the right, flowing beyond sight toward Superior. They sat on a shelf of black-veined bedrock and watched it go.

"When I was five or six," Gun said, "I'd hike back here. I had a little cane fishing pole. I'd sit on this rock all morning with a mayfly on my hook."

"By yourself? Pretty brave kid. No, brave parents."

"Not really. It looks wild, but if you grow up in a place, then I guess it's yours. It never seemed scary."

She nodded at the calm water. There were slow whorls on its surface, the water turning, considering which direction to take. "Ever catch anything?"

"No, there's nothing to catch. It only runs in springtime, with the melt. You don't think of that as a kid, though. I remember getting up before my parents and pulling my gear together, the pole and some tackle, leaders and number-six hooks and a few flies that Dad tied. A long rope stringer, since I was going to catch a bunch. Then while I was making a sandwich Dad would usually come out from the bedroom and start making coffee. I think he got a bang out of it, his kid going off so serious."

"But he didn't come with you?"

"Nope. I never expected it, or really wanted it. But I liked having him see me off. He'd say Be careful, boy, and I'd ask him"—Gun grinned—"I'd ask, 'Are there wolverines, Dad?' because I'd heard the stories. And he'd say no, he didn't believe it was the right time of year for wolverines. And away I'd go."

It was still cool, and more so on the rock, but Carol was unlacing her boots. She slipped her feet free and laid them pink-stockinged in his lap. "They're cold," she said. "What stories?"

"Wolverine stories." He picked up her feet in his hands, held them, rubbed their high arches with his thumbs. "They're smart animals. They have a vengeful reputation."

"Mmmm, scary."

Her smile was so unburdened he thought of his daughter, Mazy, her eyes full of lights at the suggestion of stories. Mazy at, say, the age of ten.

"Okay, this really happened. There was an old guy, I never knew his name. A trapper. He had a cabin not far from here, and he took mink, marten, fox, whatever came along. One morning he went out and there was a big timber wolf in one of his traps. A big white one, gorgeous, the kind that was worth a lot of money then."

Her eyes played with him. "This is before the animal-rights movement?"

"People then didn't have time for hobbies."

"Philistine."

He smiled. He rubbed her feet. "The wolf was a beauty, but it was worthless—it was all torn up, the hide ripped and some of the body eaten away. A wolverine did it. They're not as big as a wolf, but much nastier. The trapper was furious. So he laid half a dozen big traps around the carcass, thinking the critter would come back to the kill."

"And did it?"

"Sure it did. It came back that night and smelled the traps, probably laughed its head off. Tiptoed right in among them and ate the rest of the wolf, then found the trapper's prints in the snow and followed them back to his cabin."

"Gun, is this really true?"

"In the morning, now, the trapper dresses up warm and slings his pack over his shoulder, he's got his rifle along and can't wait to get out and see if he caught the wolverine. Except by this time the beast is up on the guy's roof. Right over the door."

"Ah!"

"He was locking up when it dropped on him. Later they found his key, still in the door." Gun went to a whisper. "That, and a mitten. That's all they found. Feet warm?"

She leaned in and kissed him, twice, her lips soft and understanding his exactly. She moved up into his lap, and he breathed the light cinnamon of her hair at his neck; and the sun rose higher, drawing a shimmer of mist from the water and warming their bit of bedrock at last, and her feet also.

Walking back through willows, she asked again, "Was any of it true, Gun?"

"Every syllable," he answered. She was holding his hand. What could be better?


Gunsten was sitting grim upon the porch when they got back, his face cut into a scowl. Madilyn was next to him, and Gun had the irritating feeling they'd just fallen quiet, seeing him and Carol. The morning was warming quickly now, the sun magnified through humidity, but Madilyn still wore a blanket over her shoulders. Gunsten was in pressed pants and a green corduroy suit jacket—visiting clothes.

No one spoke until they reached the porch, and then it was Carol. "Is Neb worse this morning?"

"I don't really know," Gunsten said. "He wasn't at the hospital, so I just don't know."

"What? He's checked out already?"

"Nope, he's not checked out. He just *walked* out, it looks like. Upsetting his nurses." Gunsten peered up through owly brows. "I stopped by his house. Nora's all edgy. She was going off to look for him."

"What's going on, Dad?"

Gunsten shook his head.

Carol spoke. "Gun and I'll go look for him. Any ideas?"

"I'll go, too," Gunsten said.

"Dad, stay here. Stay with Mom."

"No, it's fine," Madilyn said. Her voice was as hard as Gun had ever heard it. "Go with them. It'll be easier than having you here."

The telephone rang inside the house. Nobody wanted to get it. Gun moved first.

"Gun? It's Green. Listen now: Neb Summers was just here. I think I hit him pretty hard." He said it so quick Gun wasn't sure what he was hearing.

"Back up, Green. What's going on? What did he want? Where'd he go?"

"Another note came. For money—a lot this time. He always thought it was me—"

So Neb *was* being blackmailed. "Green, I have to know everything you can tell me. Slow down and tell it so I can understand you."

Over the phone he could hear Green's breathing, could imagine the janitor's mattery eyes closing, trying to round up some calm. Then: "Three notes came, oh, in the last three years. Somebody saying they knew about him killing Harry."

"And because you saw him, you were the obvious choice."

"He came to my place after the first one. 'Fifteen thousand dollars,' he said, 'Who you think you're messin' with?' I didn't know what th' hell he meant. He said he knew it was me, and how could I be so damn stupid? *Armp.* I tol' him I didn't want nothin'. Maybe he believed me. But he hit me then, sure as hell. Hard. Couple times, too. Beating up an ol' man."

"What happened this morning?"

"He came in, now he's walkin' funny. Tol' me he had a stroke. Is that true?"

"It's true."

"I shouldn'ta swung at him, then."

"What'd he say?"

"Well, he was back to thinkin' it was me. I guess he didn't have nobody else. 'I don't have the money,' he yells, and I say, 'Oh, how much'm I askin' for this time?' And he hollers, 'You know damn well, it's fifty.'"

"Fifty thousand?"

"Lotta money for an ol' cop."

"Did he say where he was going?"

"He called me bastard, and I hit him. On the mouth. He didn't say nothin' when he left."

"Listen, Green. If he comes back, don't let him in."

"Everyone think ol' Green's a dummy."

# 29

They checked Neb's house first. Empty. Nora had evidently gone looking for her husband. She'd taken the Buick.

"Does Neb have another car?" Carol said.

"Just the police car, and Henry's got that. Neb's probably walking."

"Then he shouldn't be too hard to find. Copper Strike's a small town."

Gunsten said, "That doesn't mean much. I suspect he'll be found when he wants to be."

Carol was riding in the front seat of the Dodge, next to Gun. "I don't understand. He's had a mild stroke. He threatened Green, even though he must have known Green wasn't blackmailing him. Maybe he's disoriented."

Gun circled the block on which Green lived, a block of slatted wood and asphalt houses with roofs that showed their ribs. The morning had turned graceful with sun and a clean breeze from the west. Twice they saw people walking, out purely for the weather, people whose eyes and appreciative faces said there could be no evil about on a morning like this.

Gunsten sat in the backseat and said nothing.

A slow cruise on the streets between Green's neighborhood and Neb's showed them nothing new. They went on for a while without direction. People sat on their porches in painted metal chairs or raked up winter debris in their meager front yards. Their movements were measured and slow and full of gratitude for spring.

They drove the length of Copper Strike and then its breadth, ending up outside the city limits before turning around and driving back in. HOME OF GUN PEDERSEN. It made him ache a little, how proud they'd been of him. How infrequently he'd come back home. His father's presence in the car made him wonder when his parents had last visited him in Minnesota. A long time back. Amanda had been alive then.

Henry Littenen was just leaving the Law Enforcement Center in the Taurus patrol car when Gun pulled into the lot. He and Gun spoke through rolled-down windows.

"Where you headed, Henry?"

"Over to Neb's. I went there first thing this morning, but Nora told me he was gone. I drove around town already. Got skunked."

"Us, too."

"I've been making a few calls. He hasn't been back to the hospital, Cal hasn't seen him. I even thought he might've gone to see Hunter Watson, though what good's a lawyer to him now I don't know. Hunter was still in bed."

"You think Neb's gone back home?"

"Not really. Nobody's answering the phone, but I guess that could be intentional." Henry started rolling up the window. "Guess I don't know where else to go."

As the Taurus turned onto the street Carol said, "Maybe we should head home. We can't do much else."

But Gun for some reason was thinking otherwise, and so, apparently, was his father. "Son? Would you mind following Henry?"

Gun U-turned in the police lot and did so, aware of Carol's curious stare. He wanted to explain to her what he was doing but knew he couldn't. His brain felt full of low clouds and uncertainty, his only clarity the consciousness of his fingers on the wheel, following Henry Littenen at a procrastinating pace toward the Summers house. He experienced a vague and sickly understanding, a premonition made up of history and landscape and God knew what else, as if a soiled wind had blown in across the town and offered him knowledge he did not want. He adjusted the rearview and looked back at his father. Gunsten met his eyes and held them.

Nora still hadn't returned and no one answered when Henry rang the doorbell. He rang it again, pressing the button until they could hear the chime like a church bell calling on a faraway Easter morning. The door was locked. The chime faded, leaving them there on the sidewalk with the sun up and stretching to summer. In an overgrown juniper by the door a lone chickadee made frantic dashes, its wings shuffling through greenery. Then a sound like a demolition explosive drummed the earth at their feet, one deep percussion, a golden wind chime swayed and tinkled over the door and Henry grabbed at the locked knob, pawed at it like a crazy pup until Gun shoved him sideways and gave the door his fully committed shoulder, the dead bolt holding but the hinges giving way and Gun tumbling over the jamb and landing painfully on a fresh bronze screw. They flooded the entrance while he got to his feet, Gunsten calling "Neb!" and Henry running to where he knew the bedrooms were until Carol knelt down and put their attention on the floor.

The slug, twelve-gauge, manufactured for deer, had stopped just as its mushroomed head broke through the hardwood floor. It looked like a silver-gray beetle emerging from a bed of splinters. Carol put out a finger as if to touch it, then drew back and folded her arms around herself. No one else moved until Henry said, his voice dry and bare as sand, "I'll have to go downstairs now. Gun, I'd appreciate it if you'd come with me."

# 30

*God am I sorry.*

That's what Neb Summers had written, in pencil, on a piece of Nora's lavender stationery. He'd come back from Green's, apparently found his wife gone, and come down to the basement. His guns were all here, in a tan metal cabinet, its door a handspan open. Mostly rifles. A Winchester thirty-thirty, a .308 also by Winchester, a .222 Swift, an old J.C. Higgins .22 for woodchucks and ravens. There was one handgun, Neb's police .38, holstered. And his shotgun, the Remington 12 he'd favored for whitetails, and which he'd chosen this morning for the job at hand.

He'd sat down upon an overturned five-gallon pail and used the narrow end of his nightstick to push the trigger.

A layer of smoke rode like fog on the air, chest-high and smelling of sulfur and nitrate. There were other smells. The heavy decaying odor of a body emptying

itself of waste, the salt-metal bite of blood, the dusty
taste of powdered gypsum still sifting down from the
hole in the ceiling. Around the hole, and on the wall
nearest it, the Sheetrock was as liquid as a slaughter-
house pen, light reflecting from it like from a wet ruby
mirror.

The floor creaked above them, and the stairway
door opened. Carol called, "Gun?"

"Stay upstairs, you and Dad."

He heard the door swing shut and her slow footsteps
traversing the floor. Henry was kneeling beside Neb,
who'd landed on his back with the tipped bucket
between his knees. Cranial matter slid down the
liquid wall behind him. Neb's clothes were simple
police wear, blue shirt, creased black pants, thick-
soled black shoes. His left wrist wore a hospital ID
band.

The back of Gun's throat tasted sour. He forced his
eyes from the body. The room was apparently Neb's
den. There was a single armchair, upholstered in a
clean blue-and-white check, a low maple cabinet
containing several years' subscriptions to *Fur, Fish &
Game* and another next to it with police manuals,
criminal psychology, and a hardcover with a faded
blue jacket titled *Man Tracks: Hunting the Fugitive*.
Next to the bannister was a small maple desk with a
green banker's light on it. A carved heron with poised
beak and lifted leg stood under the light. The heron
was standing on Neb's farewell.

*God am I sorry.*

And in the top desk drawer, lying atop a mess of
paid water and light bills, was a blackmail letter.

It was in handprinted capitals on cheap white stock,
ripped at the edge. Gun didn't pick it up. He read it
quietly, felt something go dark inside him like a movie
ending in the wrong place, and said, "Henry," leaving
the drawer open.

I HERE YOU ARE DYING SOON SO THIS
IS THE LAST PAYMENT YOU'LL HAVE TO
MAKE. FIFTY THOUSAND THIS TIME AND
ITS YOUR DAM GOOD FORTUNE I DONT
ASK A LOT MORE. LEAVE IT THE SAME
PLACE AS BEFORE.

"Ah, Lord," Henry said. He had the note in his
hand. It was written on a mostly blank page torn from
some publication. Large format. Some sort of hand-
book or manual. It went on:

IF YOU GET TOO CURIOUS REMEMBER
HOW HARD LIFE WILL GET FOR SWEET
BOY CALVIN. KILLER CALVIN. GOD-DAM
CALVIN. IT WAS BAD FOR YOU WHO BUR-
IED THAT KID, THINK HOW BAD FOR HIM
WHAT DID THE KILLING.

Henry said, *"Calvin* killed Harry? Is that what it
says?"
"That's what it sounds like." Gun peered at the
back of the note. It was a page cut from an old
Peterson auto manual. A footer in capitals said TIM-
ING BELT REPLACEMENT.
"And then Neb covered," Henry said. "Buried his
own nephew, then covered for his son. If this is true."
"Yeah." Gun felt his stomach move. If the note
wasn't true, would Neb have eaten a slug? "You're the
law, Henry. I'm going upstairs."
Gunsten looked tight-faced and old, getting the
news, his expression not changing the while, his long
hands calm on the arms of a tall rocker in Neb's living
room. Carol's eyes looked handslapped, but she
wasn't crying.
"Sounds like Henry better talk to Calvin," Gunsten
said.

"Or whoever wrote that note." Gun closed his eyes. Just days ago it had seemed like nobody knew what happened to Harry; now it seemed a number of folks had known all along, and the club kept growing. Now, a blackmailer with bad spelling.

"Green Tokannah?"

"Not Green. I'd bet against it." Gun remembered the janitor's ruinous face, the gruff voice telling the story and the eyes backing it up all the way. Still, who else would have seen the murder? Who'd have seen *Calvin* kill Harry Summers with a hammer, and then stuck around while Neb buried him?

And the note itself: Would Neb have left it there to condemn his own son?

It didn't reason.

Behind him a cuckoo clock snapped and struck, the red-mouthed bird popping out annoyingly, endlessly, eleven times. It stopped, there was quiet, and the telephone rang.

Carol answered. "Summers residence." She waited, her lips going thin, and covered the phone with one hand. "It's the hospital. Nora Summers is there, saying she's been all over town looking for her husband. She's furious they let him get away."

"It's your call," Gun said. Behind Carol's hand he could hear a voice cheeping anxiously, a jittery finch.

Carol nodded. She uncovered the phone and said, "You have Mrs. Summers there? Good. I think you better check her in."

When Madilyn had absorbed all they could tell her, the information seeming to bleach her skin and stiffen her joints, Gun left the house and went to the barn. The Indian was where his father had left it, parked on a piece of canvas spread over the dirt floor. Gunsten's motorcycle tools, thin-handled Brukker wrenches and a small collection of sockets, had been wiped clean and returned to their pegs above the workbench. The barn was dim and smelled of remnant exhaust, old oil, and the light dry dirt of the floor, so flour-fine with age it would hold spilled water in a glossy bead. The narrow block of sun in the doorway looked warm, the day keeping its promise to be good; but Gun remembered when the barn had seemed big enough to hold all the bad weather the Peninsula could handle. He remembered being afraid, when his father would kick-start the Indian and bring it grumbling out, toes touching for balance on both sides, that the darkness of the barn would issue from it like a stream of sparrows, disperse in a rush to the corners of his bright world, then rise from every horizon in banks of brown cloud.

The motorcycle started on the fourth kick, and Gun walked it out in neutral, straddling the seat. It appeared healthy, a good idle, no sudden failures or screaming accelerations, and he stepped it into gear and rode out of the yard.

He rode, as Gunsten did, without a helmet, the wind pushing his cheekbones tight and putting water in his eyes. The bike was responsive to throttle though not quick in jackrabbit fashion because the speed took time to build, burgeon, carry along all that weight. It was a porker with big shoulders, the truest of hogs, and Gun fed it gas until everything along the highway —the lichen-etched bedrock hills, the stretches of tall grass blocked with stands of basswood and maple and lacy pines that leaned out over the road—froze solid in his vision into flat colored walls on either side of him, the pictures there like slashes of paint from a reckless brush.

He supposed it was always the lake that drew him, as it drew thousands of others. Growing up near Superior you took it for granted, like God, you assumed its icy proximity, you dived in on the rare hot days and came up screeching. When he'd lost Amanda he'd gone to live next to water, to a smaller lake that nonetheless reminded him of this one. When the days started bouncing you too hard, you went to the water and dove for a blessing.

He parked the Indian behind a jut of greenstone the size of an outhouse and peered down at the lake. It was a fair drop, probably thirty feet. It wasn't too steep, though, and from here the road went back up to higher ground, away from the water. Gun knelt and untied his shoes, old Pony runners shot long ago. He removed his socks and then peeled to the waist. As always it was cooler at the shore and the perpetual mist sealed around him as he turned and started down, toes and fingers holding to stone.

At the bottom he stepped out on a table of rock where the waves spread themselves into ripples. He felt his skin contract and his breath go shallow. Looking up he saw the rock he'd descended, the bike sitting above him, a thin reach of cloud in the north. He stripped off his pants and tossed them partway up the slope, then turned and made note of a small stone island a ways out. A couple hundred yards. There were two seagulls sitting there, and not room for many more.

The water smoked with cold.

# 31

Morning came in full of pale Peninsula sunlight that painted the kitchen walls with a field of yellow flax. You threw parties over such mornings here, but breakfast this time was quiet. And huge: Madilyn had stayed up past midnight to roll out the overnight cinnamon buns, and this morning before dawn Gun had listened to her in the kitchen below, opening and closing the squealing oven door, whisking buckwheat batter, setting the table with the blue and white Currier and Ives plates she saved for important or, as in this case, diversionary meals. There was ham, griddle-fried, and scrambled eggs, hash browns straight from the potato by way of Madilyn's hand-crank grinder. Way too much to eat.

Except for pleasantries about food and weather, no one said much until Gunsten pushed his plate away, tossed his napkin from his lap to the table, and announced he was going fishing.

This was Gunsten's way of responding to bad or puzzling news: go off and brood, find a place to go figure for a while. Gun didn't fault him.

"Why not take somebody along?" said Madilyn—after all these years, still not at peace with her man's solitary ways.

"I'd love to go," Carol said. She had a coating of Madilyn's powdered-sugar frosting on her lips. Bless her, Gun thought.

Gunsten bit his lip and threw a hard look at his wife, who threw it back it even harder.

"Unless you'd rather go alone," Carol said.

"No, that's fine." Gunsten stood, dusting crumbs from the front of his flannel shirt. "Five minutes, and dress warm."

Gun stuck around to help his mother with the dishes and talk, not that there was much to be said. They'd stayed up into the night, all of them, visiting in the living room about the end of Neb Summers and the surprise he'd left behind, which no one could make sense of. If Neb's wife and Green Tokannah were both coming clean, and Gun believed they were, then it looked as if Neb was simply making a story to clear his own name in death. A frightening prospect—a man trying to throw guilt on his only son. What kind of a man did a thing like that?

Madilyn tossed a handful of rinsed silverware into the drain rack. "It's hard for me to believe that of him," she said. "Putting it on Calvin that way. I can see Neb keeping a secret. I can even see him killing somebody—maybe. But doing such a thing to his own boy? You have to shudder for the man's soul."

Gun started to dry the silverware and put it away. "I guess I don't believe it."

"So you think Calvin *did* do it?"

"I'm just saying I don't think Neb would try and

shift blame at a time like that. You're putting an end to yourself, you don't start telling stories."

"Gun, if Neb killed his own nephew all those years ago, he'd been telling stories a long, long time. His scruples were flattened to dust."

They finished the dishes, and Gun drove into Copper Strike. His mind, for now, had let go of Neb and taken up instead the picture of blond Rick Dandrie, lying drowned in a ditch, his poor teased hair all matted to hell, his blood full of booze. Gun remembered the unfriendly exchange he'd witnessed between Dandrie and Calvin Summers that night at Speed Ruona's bar. If there had been any blackmailing going on, Dandrie might not be a bad place to start looking. Too bad the man could no longer speak for himself.

Gun didn't so much decide where to go as he simply ended up there. It was the only place he'd seen the two men together. This morning a single car was parked out front, a mid-eighties Grand Am, black; Rufus Summers's.

The man was sitting at the bar with coffee, watching the "Today" show, Speed Ruona atop the stool next to him. Bryant Gumbel smiled stupidly at something Katie Couric had just said; she was blushing.

Speed Ruona glanced up at Gun and made a coffee-pouring motion with his hand, a help-yourself. Which Gun did. He sat down on the other side of Rufus, leaving an empty stool between them. "Morning," he said.

"My head still hurts, thanks to you. Good morning." Rufus turned and smiled with half his mouth, those cool eyes gleaming away inside his head.

"You're still here," Gun said. "Thought you'd be back in Chicago."

"I was till last night. Looks like another funeral in the family."

"Sorry about your uncle."

"Me, too."

"Can we talk?" Gun asked.

"What, about Neb?"

"Calvin."

"It'll ruin my day," said Rufus.

Speed Ruona got up from his stool and stretched his arms back in a way that made his chest arch outward. "You guys watch the place for a while. I gotta go upstairs. Morning weights."

"Huh?" said Rufus.

"I lift, mornings," Speed said. Rufus scanned down old Speed Ruona's torso and nodded; the man had on a T-shirt that put sense in his words. Speed disappeared through the door that led upstairs to his apartment.

Gun picked up the remote and clicked off the television just as Willard Scott's mountainous self appeared, grinning amidst a sea of children. Willard shrank and went black with the screen.

"I like that weatherman," Rufus complained.

"Me, too," said Gun. "But I'm wondering what you can tell me about Dandrie. You know, the guy they found last week in the ditch. What about him and Calvin?"

"What about them?"

"They knew each other."

"Sure, but why're you asking me, and why should I talk?" Rufus had the sly-cat look on his face. His body seemed relaxed yet at the same time jammed full with energy.

"I've got a lot more to gain than you've got to lose."

"Probably," said Rufus, smiling. "Try again."

"I'm bigger than you," Gun said.

Rufus laughed. "I do a lot of work for people who *aren't* bigger than me."

"I could pay . . . though I'd rather not."

"We *are* talking family here. I got my principles."

"You heard about the note, I suppose."

Rufus nodded, his pointed pink tongue poking at the corner of his mouth. "The note that said Calvin was the guy? Yeah, Henry told me about it."

"A man in your kind of business, I'd think you'd be curious."

Rufus sipped his coffee, listening, nervous electricity leaking out one of his little fingers, which drummed the bar.

"You might consider Neb's good name," said Gun. "I get the feeling you liked him."

Rufus jerked his head to one side and rotated his shoulder socket, getting himself loose. He said, "Something ain't right."

"I'm with you, buddy. That's why I'd like to hear what you know about this Dandrie fellow."

"What I know you could get from anyone," said Rufus. "Kids on the street, anybody with a sense for what's up. Guys like that, it's almost like a civic job."

"What, he was selling dope?"

"He moved a lot of shit around up here—Houghton, Hancock, all over the peninsula. Calvin helped him sometimes, went to Chicago on pickups pretty regular, even got a wild hair every so often and went out on his own. You know . . . invest a little, make a little."

"What, Calvin would buy from Dandrie, then sell it himself?"

"Like I said, every so often. Mostly just made trips or delivered goods to the scum down the food chain. Rick Dandrie made it worth his time—just barely."

"Do you think Neb knew anything about it? Or Henry Littenen?"

"I don't know how they couldn't. The way I see it for Dandrie, working with Calvin had its perks, if you get what I mean."

"Protection," said Gun.

"Strong word there," said Rufus. "Let's just say with Cal in the picture Dandrie didn't have to be so careful. Neb was a proud daddy."

Gun drank some coffee. He said, "The night I saw him and Calvin in here they were at odds. Dandrie was flexing a little. Any idea why?"

Rufus yawned. "Just a collection matter, if I was gonna guess."

"You're guessing?"

Rufus shrugged and looked straight up toward the sound coming from upstairs, a man grunting, the soft clank of steel weights. "Calvin took some shit a month or two ago on IOU. Dandrie seemed to think it was past due."

"Didn't Calvin get the stuff sold?"

"That wouldn't have been the catch, Gun. For Cal, the catch would've been hanging onto his take long enough to make good on the loan. You can bet he didn't take long selling it."

"Expensive habits?"

"Nah, Jim Beam's always been plenty for Calvin. It's just . . . he makes money disappear. Like last month he flies off to Florida for a couple weeks to see an old pal. Plane fare, nice room, good food, a broad or two, you know, and the scoots are gone. He comes back here, and Dandrie wants to see his loan. Problem, though. Dandrie's sort of new around town, and word is he fancies himself a tough guy. And Calvin, the way I see it, he's been spoiled over the years by hometown forgiveness. He's not used to being pushed."

"What are you saying?" Gun asked.

"Hypothesizing," said Rufus.

"You think Calvin had to push back?"

"I honestly couldn't say."

Gun tried to decide if this connection worked for

him. Say Calvin *had* killed Dandrie over a loan. Say his money problems with Dandrie had gone on for some time. Would he have blackmailed his dad to stay afloat?

"I'm not sure what to think," Gun said. "What about you, Rufus?"

"Me either."

"Tell me. Do you put any stock in the note we found in Neb's desk? You've known Calvin all your life. You think he killed Harry, and then Neb protected him all this time?"

"I doubt it."

"How'd the two of them get along when they were kids, Calvin and Harry?" Gun asked. "Calvin told me Harry was always the golden boy, first-string everything. A little resentment, I'd say. And Calvin went off to Nam, too. . . ."

Their coffee was dry and Rufus got up to fix the situation, glided around the end of the bar and poured out the last from the stainless steel coffee maker. Upstairs the grunting and clanking went on. "Charles Atlas," said Rufus, his eyes going to the ceiling.

Gun had the bottom of the pot, chewy. He waited for Rufus to get comfortable again. He could sense the man working up to something.

"An interesting thing," Rufus started. "About Vietnam and shit. A week or so ago, just before Harry got found, Calvin stopped at my place in Chicago. He was having car problems and needed help, so we drank and worked on that damn Chevy half the night. Got it fixed, too, the timing chain. Lucky for us he had an old Peterson manual for that year. . . ."

Gun felt all the switches going on inside his brain, but he tried not to let his face show it. He nodded and told his eyes to stay quiet and be serious.

"He was talking about Nam, though," Rufus was saying. "You ask me what it was like between Harry

213

and him? Well, that night he said he figured Harry wasn't so dumb after all. He said that war over there was a damn poor excuse for a war." Rufus sipped his coffee. "Never heard him say anything like it before. Calvin'll go off the track to nail a peace hound or anybody that questions what happened in the jungle. Then again, he was drunk, too, that night."

"Making his peace with Harry?" Gun asked—but his thoughts had moved well on down the road, already searching out the car repair manual with the missing page.

"Whatever that means," said Rufus. "Maybe he's just lookin' at himself and how he turned out, and thinking, 'How the hell did this happen?'"

Gun felt himself smiling, thinking *Thank you, thank you, Rufus.*

# 32

At ten-thirty that evening Gun's parents stood up from their matching cedar chairs and said good night. They looked years older than they had just days ago when Gun and Carol had arrived. Madilyn, normally straight-spined and sharp of eye, was bent and squinting. She had on the glasses she usually wore for reading only, and her crisp blue eyes were red-veined. Gunsten was sagging at the shoulders. The deep pockets beneath his cheekbones gave the mistaken impression that he was not well-fed.

"Don't stay up late now," said Madilyn. "You both look tired."

"Thanks for a wonderful day," Carol said. "Gunsten, I love your lake." She leaned back against Gun on the couch, relaxed within the semicircle of his arm, none of the tightness in her back, no muscles doing overtime in her jaw.

"It sure ain't mine." Gunsten smiled at her. He and Carol had gotten in from fishing at suppertime, wind-burned and easy with each other, Carol holding a stringer of lake trout shining and ready for the knife.

Gun said, "Carol and I might go for a little drive. So if you hear us leave . . ."

"It's late—" said Madilyn, but Gunsten was turning her around and heading her toward the stairs.

"You kids have fun," said Gun's dad over his shoulder.

The lake beneath Stiller's Lookout was dark and mild-mannered, but the small eastern breeze seemed to be on the rise, and the smell it brought promised change. Gun and Carol sat on the edge of the high bank, listening to the swells die in the large rocks below. There was a lot of black night around and ahead of them, but Gun would have been glad for even more. They didn't speak, words seeming a feeble substitute for the things that mattered.

At two A.M. they left Stiller's Lookout and drove toward Calvin's place. This afternoon Gun had described to Carol his conversation with Rufus, and for now, they'd decided, there was no point in saying anything to his parents or anyone else. It seemed wiser to lay hands on the confirming evidence first. Then it might be time to go see Henry Littenen or the state police.

The lights were all off in Calvin's little house, and the Chevy was not parked in the driveway. Either Calvin was gone or he'd put his car in the garage. Gun drove a block farther down the street, took a right, and parked next to a lilac hedge gone wild. There were no streetlights close by. He and Carol walked back toward Calvin's through the alley and came into the yard the back way.

216

"You think we'll have to break in?" Carol whispered.

Gun shook his head. He doubted if Calvin bothered to lock up. No one else did.

They were standing at the south end of the garage, and Gun had to go up on his toes to look inside the small high window. He saw the Chevy parked inside. Good. Unhappily, though, a streetlight lit the alley in front of Calvin's garage, and they had no choice but to stand smack in the middle of its white glare as they tried the side door, which indeed was open.

"At least there's no dogs awake in the neighborhood," Gun said. "Knock on wood."

"Or insomniac old men, let's hope," Carol said.

Gun took a deep breath and squeezed Carol by the shoulder. She felt cold.

The Chevy took up most of the single-car garage, and as luck would have it, Calvin *had* bothered to lock up. Probably a habit picked up on his business trips to Chicago. For a moment Gun imagined Calvin standing at a blue postal drop-box on a Chicago street, taking a last look at the letter he'd addressed in block letters to disguise his hand. Was he proud of his artwork? Did he think himself shrewd? Did he think Neb really *had* the fifty grand? Was it funny to him, knowing Green Tokannah was the guy Neb would blame? And what did Green Tokannah know? Apparently not quite everything about that miserable night.

For Gun to open the car door with the coat hanger he'd brought took ten minutes, long enough for the police to have shown up if someone had spotted them entering the garage. Another five minutes and they'd searched the car, finding plenty of stuff, but no Peterson repair manual. In the trunk was a forgotten bag of groceries—sour milk, rotten tomatoes, a bag of chocolate chip cookies—and a bunch of aluminum beer empties. Underneath the front seat rode a .45

automatic. A little too much pop for rodents. And the ashtray held a roll of bills, fifties and twenties. Carol counted six hundred dollars. She rolled the bills tight again and stuffed them back in.

"This guy's a mess," she said. "I can't believe he had it together enough to throw that stupid book away."

"He probably didn't. Let's check his tool bench."

Light from the street lamp filtered in through the windows and allowed for an easy search of Calvin's garage. The tool bench, such as it was, gave them nothing. An odd assortment of power tools, old rusty wrenches and screwdrivers, nuts and bolts, a few bags of nails, everything randomly thrown together. Underneath the bench were piles of catalogs for hunting and fishing gear. No car repair manual. After half an hour of searching they gave up.

Back in Gun's rented Dodge the digital clock showed three o'clock. Carol said, "I was sure we'd find it. Positive."

"I was pretty sure myself." Gun started the Dodge and pushed the temperature lever all the way over to the right. The east wind had continued to rise, cooling the night way down. Gun expected rain by dawn. He looked over at Carol, sitting with her bare arms wrapped around herself. "I hope you're up for one more stop," he said.

"You're always so much fun, Pedersen."

Gun swung the Dodge into a U-turn, jumped the curb with one tire, and headed back toward the center of town. There wouldn't be light for another hour and a half; with rain moving in, maybe longer. "My patience has about had it," said Gun.

"Yeah?"

"Because I thought of something just now." He was surprised he hadn't thought of it sooner. "We're trying to get our minds around the idea of a guy blackmailing his own dad, right?"

"Which it looks like he was, Gun. And for *protecting* him. You'd think Calvin'd be so grateful he wouldn't be able to get up off his knees."

"Let's say Neb came up with that money, the fifty thousand, and handed it over."

"I doubt it," said Carol.

"Just speculating. We know that great uncle Max sent him something, though we don't know how much. And Neb probably had resources of his own. It doesn't matter if he put together the whole package. Just say he got a pile of it and handed it off. What's Calvin going to do with it?" Gun was turning onto Main Street now, and it was dead, nothing moving anywhere. He drove the length of the business district, was satisfied by the quiet, and turned back again. Calvin's real estate office was on the north side, a small wood-frame building squeezed between two larger brick structures. New white paint covered the fake-brick tarpaper. The sign said SUMMERS LAND OFFICE, CALVIN SUMMERS: OWNER AND LICENSED AGENT.

"You're thinking if Cal got a chunk of money, he might not be sticking around for long," said Carol.

Gun nodded. "I'm thinking it's time to push him. Nail him before his dad's funeral."

"How?"

"Like you were saying, Carol. It's hard to believe Calvin had it together enough to throw away that book."

"You think he's got it here in his office?"

Gun shrugged. "Not really."

He parked around back of the realty building, and they sat in the car for a few minutes to see if they'd attracted any notice. It was dark there, and Calvin's small office was set in from the adjoining buildings in a way that cut it off from view up and down the alley.

"Are we going to sit here or go inside?" asked Carol.

Gun opened his door quietly and stepped out. Carol slid quickly over the driver's seat and got out the same side. Her eyes were burning away like small green mantles, and her breathing was coming faster now. "You don't enjoy this too much, do you?" Gun whispered.

The back door was windowless and locked with a dead bolt that would require more battering than Gun was prepared to dole out. The only window in the back wall was Plexiglas.

"Hey." Carol was poking her foot into a heavy growth of weeds and tree shoots at the base of the foundation. She knelt down and reached into the stuff with one hand. "There's a window well in here. Not very big, though."

They yanked out weeds and bent aside the tree shoots to expose the small basement window. "Big enough for you, I bet," Gun said.

"Oh, great."

Sitting with his rear end braced against the edge of the window well, Gun didn't have any trouble forcing the window with his feet, snapping the lock. Stale, dank air rose from the basement.

He lowered Carol in feet first. It was a little tight at the hips and shoulders. Gun handed down a small flashlight, then waited at the back door longer than he expected to until the deadbolt clicked open.

"Sorry," she told him. "Filthy bathroom."

Inside there were just two other rooms. A large one with a desk, three file cabinets, and a few lumpy easy chairs, and a smaller waiting area with well-worn sectional furniture. They searched the desk first and found very little of anything. Pens, paper clips, a few brand-new legal pads, some business cards printed with SUMMERS LAND COMPANY, a carton of Baby Ruth candy bars, and a file marked "Current Listings," which held half a dozen Polaroid snapshots of properties, each one stapled to a single sheet of descriptive information. The file cabinets held even less evidence of Calvin's sales acumen. They were empty.

"His competition must be trembling," said Carol.

"He's not paying the bills this way."

"Does he spend any time in here, I wonder?"

"I've seen him coming in and out."

The waiting room magazines scattered on the central table covered an impressive range: *Wee Wisdom*, *Penthouse*, *Sports Afield*, *Reader's Digest*, *Self*, *Newsweek*. There were magazines stacked on a corner bookshelf, too. No Peterson manuals.

"We're not going to find it," Gun said, walking back into the larger room. He sat down at the desk and opened the top drawer.

"You weren't expecting to." Carol dropped into one of the easy chairs and sprawled in it. "I'm tired, Gun. What are you thinking?"

"Here, have some energy." He tossed a Baby Ruth, and Carol caught it above her head with one hand. He tore open one for himself and took a bite. "It seems to me," he said, chewing the candy bar, "that it doesn't much matter if we find the book or not. What matters is that he thinks we have."

"Maybe he knows where it is, though. Or maybe he burned the thing up."

"I doubt it. Even if he did, all we've got to do is let him know we're convinced that letter came from him. That should be enough."

"Enough to what?" asked Carol.

"Make him nervous, force him into doing something." Gun scooted forward in the cushy four-wheeled desk chair and leaned his elbows on the desk.

"I'm tired of hanging around here sniffing old bones. I'm tired of talking to people that don't know how to tell the truth anymore. I want to go home and see if the walleyes are biting off the point." He waited a long moment. "Oh, and I guess we've got some unfinished business, too, you and me?" He saw Carol's teeth in the darkness and knew she had on the smile that always made him swallow hard.

He bounced the heels of his hands against the edge of the desk.

"What do you propose?" Carol asked.

"In baseball it's called manufacturing runs. Scrapping. It's late in the game, nobody's hitting worth a damn, so you start bunting and running. If you're just a little bit lucky, they make a mistake or two. It's what you have to do to win sometimes."

"We scare the man too much and he might run," said Carol.

"Sure, but he might run anyway. I'm saying let's take the game to him now. What's there to lose? If he runs, we chase him." Gun took a pen and legal pad from the drawer. The message he left on Calvin's desk was brief.

You're missing a page Calvin. Hope that Chevy's timing belt holds up.

Gun Pedersen

# 33

The morning was vintage U.P. gray, low skies that made a guy six and a half feet tall want to walk bent-kneed to keep from plunging his head up into sloppy clouds. Nice weather if you were big on duck-hunting or checkers. But with duck season three months off, they had to settle for checkers—Gun, Carol, Madilyn, Gunsten, all of them sitting around the kitchen table, two games going continuously, a round-robin tournament. Gun had lost twice already against no wins.

He looked up at the clock above the refrigerator. Ten-thirty. Carol moved her face slightly to catch his eye. Her lips moved. *Tell them,* she was saying.

Gun nodded. He'd been hoping for an early call from Calvin, something to fill in the picture a little more before trying to describe it to his parents. But the phone had been silent. He could see Calvin about now, boarding a plane for the Bahamas. Likely, though, he was just sleeping in. Or maybe cleaning and loading the .45 he kept beneath the front seat of his Chevy. . . .

Now it was too late, of course—but sitting here with his parents, playing checkers and drinking coffee, eating Madilyn's fresh orange rolls, watching his father smack the table with his fist each time he jumped one of Carol's pieces, Gun couldn't help realizing how careless he'd been, how cavalier with the safety of the people he loved. Pushing a man like Calvin into a corner wasn't the thing to do. What the hell had he been thinking about, manufacturing runs? My Lord, Pedersen, he thought, you've been alone too long.

He cleared his throat.

"Your move," said Madilyn.

"There's something I need to tell you," Gun said. "You, too, Dad."

His parents listened carefully, but Gun could tell he wasn't getting through. Gunsten continued to eat orange rolls and drink coffee, his angular face struck with a vague disbelief. Madilyn got up once to refill everyone's cup. When Gun had finished he saw Carol look from Gunsten to Madilyn and frown.

"I'm not sure if you're grasping things here," Carol said. "The danger . . . what are you thinking?"

Madilyn shook her head. "Calvin always seemed to me like such a . . . lost sort of man," said Madilyn. "Like he wanted to be tough but didn't quite have the meanness in him."

"I think you've known him too long," said Carol. "You see somebody every week for years, you don't expect something like this."

"I suppose."

Gun said, "What about you, Dad? You're not saying much."

224

Gunsten tilted his face toward his wife. "I see it the same way. On the other hand, Madilyn's always been a mite more generous in her estimation of folks than me."

"Gunsten, that's not the case," said Madilyn.

"Oh, sure it is, but you've got to remember, too, dear. People change, sometimes for good reason. Luck can snap you the wrong way in a second, and all of a sudden life is different." Gunsten paused, rubbed a hand across the stubble of one cheek. "I don't know, back then with the war and all, those two Summers kids had an excuse for going after each other. I can see it starting out, a couple of boys banging their chests together. And if somebody hurt, it was probably an accident. Some of what you're saying, though, seems a little farfetched. Like about that Dandrie fellow they found in the ditch. You're making a big jump there. Even that page from the car repair manual. Pretty iffy."

"Dad, we're not lawyers. We're not conducting a jury trial here." Gun felt himself getting defensive. Very consciously he took a bite of orange roll. He chewed it slowly.

"All right," said Gunsten.

"But he might have killed Dandrie," said Carol. "And if he did—if he was in hock to the guy up to his eyeballs, it might explain why he'd be trying to get money from his father."

Gunsten nodded, lifted his hands to his face, and rubbed his eyes with his fingertips. He sighed with all the sad strength of his big drooping shoulders. "It's bad enough having people look at me like *I'm* the one. But at least I know better. This is almost worse—Neb being turned against by his own son. I can't hardly think about it. For a father, nothing could be as bad as that. Neb didn't deserve it." Gunsten got up and walked over to the sink. He washed out his coffee cup,

225

then stared out the window at the rotten clouds. He was still a tall, powerful man, but his long white hair yellowing now from age and the callused elbow jutting from a rip in his shirt made him look like a Norse god fallen on hard times.

"Well, I doubt we have anything to be afraid of from Calvin, whatever he is, or whatever he might've done," said Madilyn. "If it's like you say, he must want to get this over with. And think, he hasn't even buried his father yet. Tomorrow's the funeral. Nora's got relatives coming in today, and I'm sure Calvin'll be over there. It's possible he might not see that note for a couple days, don't you think?"

As though in answer to Madilyn's question, the phone rang.

# 34

Pedersen's. It's Gun."

"You know who," said Calvin.

"Calling from your office, are you?"

"We've gotta talk."

"We can work that out."

"You're way off base, Pedersen. Hope you're willing to listen."

"More than," said Gun. "When do you want to meet?"

"I want to know something first. I want to know who you've been talking to. A man's got a right to know how widely he's been slandered."

"You haven't been slandered."

"You haven't talked to anybody?"

"I said you haven't been slandered, Calvin."

"Who've you been talking to?"

"When do you want to meet?"

"Your parents, then. You told them, and that woman friend of yours. Isn't that right?"

"How about this afternoon?" Gun asked.

"No, tonight, ten-thirty. Busy day, I got relatives here. We got a funeral in the family tomorrow, in case you forgot."

"Tonight, then," Gun said. "Neutral ground. Speed Ruona's?"

"Too many people there. How about my office? By now you should feel comfortable there, Pedersen."

"I don't, Calvin. The bathroom stinks, and you've got poor taste in literature. Let's say Bosky Park. Up in the bleachers." Bosky Park was the legion baseball field on the west side of town. "Nobody around there tonight," Gun said.

"Ten-thirty at Bosky Park."

"Pull into the lot," Gun told him, "right back of the grandstand. Whoever's there first waits in his car. Got it?"

"Sure."

"Then we both get out and go up into the seats. Talk."

"Sure."

"Oh, and Calvin. That .45 under your front seat? Leave it home."

There was a short silence, "I'll do that," said Calvin. "I hope you're in a listening mood. You've got it wrong about me."

"I'll listen," said Gun, and he meant it.

Calvin hung up.

The day was brutally long. Too long to fill up with checkers, long enough for Gun to second-guess himself into a severe funk. And the weather didn't get any better. The skies lifted a bit by midafternoon, only to let loose at four o'clock with a steady, hard, straight-up-and-down rain. Gun found a bucket of baseballs in the attic, carried them out to the barn, and threw into the side of a hay bale until the bale fell apart.

At the supper table Gun was irritable on the subject of how to handle Calvin Summers. In fact, he knew it couldn't be more simple; either the man had an explanation worth listening to or else he didn't, in which case Gun would have to take the matter up with the state cops. If Calvin decided to muscle things around a little bit, that would almost be a relief.

At ten-twenty he left Gunsten, Madilyn, and Carol sitting stiffly in the living room, trying to launch a conversation.

"You're not back by eleven-thirty, I'm coming out there," said Gunsten.

"And we'll call the state police," Madilyn put in.

Carol said, "You'll be fine," in a voice so false it hurt Gun to hear it.

Outside the rain was falling good and steady. No wind, the temperature about fifty-five. A cool night. Gun drove slowly into town, past Calvin's dark office, and turned left on Johnson Avenue toward the park where he'd played a few games in his time. He parked in the lot behind the concrete grandstand. There was no other car yet. He looked at his watch. Ten-twenty-eight. He rolled down his window, looked around. Listened. A loon called sadly from the small lake off beyond the green wooden outfield fence.

Gun remembered a night twenty years ago much like tonight, rain coming down hard. A legion game against Houghton, bottom of the sixth, and the ump was trying to finish out the inning before calling the game to rain. The score was one–nothing, Houghton in front, two down, and Gun was at the plate with Jimmy Prescott on third, Skunk Turpin on second. This was it.

Copper Strike's manager, Moose Granbeck— proprietor of Moose's Diner and onetime catcher in the old Northern League—counseled Gun to shorten his swing and try to poke one through the right side of the field. The first pitch from Houghton's lanky right-hander, though, looked *so* nice, coming in easy and waist-high, that Gun, who in his mind was already traversing the muddy base paths in a home-run trot, swung from the heels. He got underneath the pitch and flied out to left, ending the game. Afterward in the locker room Moose said nothing. Skunk Turpin, though, leaned over and hissed into Gun's ear: "Such a pretty swing there, Pedersen. Wow." Skunk's family lived in a one-room house without plumbing, and Gun would never forgot the sour smell of him that night in the locker room. He didn't forget, either, whenever the situation called for it, to hit the ball to the right side.

He looked again at his watch. Ten-thirty-three, still no sign of Calvin, and Gun was getting uncomfortable. Starting to squirm. His lower back was cramping, and even with the seat pushed all the way back he couldn't fully extend his legs. Glancing up in the rearview mirror he saw two pairs of headlights coming his way on Johnson Avenue. He watched as the first pair turned in and the second slowed and went on by. A late model Ford pulled up twenty feet to Gun's left. A boy and girl sitting close together in the front seat looked over wide-eyed to see who'd gotten there ahead of them. Gun waved, and the two kids backed up quickly and drove off. The other car, a dark station wagon, was out of sight already. If it was Calvin, he was driving somebody else's vehicle.

Gun waited another couple minutes. No car yet. No Calvin. What the hell was the man doing? Didn't he have the sense to get here on time? Impatient now, Gun got out and walked up the cement steps into the little stadium. He made a quick round of the grandstand to satisfy himself that no one was here, then he stood behind home plate and hung his fingers in the wire mesh of the backstop.

Yes, Gun told himself, Calvin had agreed on ten-thirty, here, and he'd sounded serious about wanting to talk. What else had been said? Gun tried to pull the conversation from his memory. Calvin had wanted to know who Gun had been talking to, and Gun had put him off. *Have you talked to your parents?* Calvin had asked. *To that woman friend of yours? Slander* was a word he'd used.

Again from the lake beyond the outfield a loon cried, but this time Gun imagined that he saw the sound rising in the rain-drenched sky like a slender stain of blood.

*Your parents—you told them and that woman friend of yours. Isn't that right?*

Gun ran from the grandstand and into the parking lot, blood pounding away at his stomach. He started up the Dodge and drove toward home as fast as the wet roads would let him.

# 35

*I*t was ten-forty-eight on the car's digital clock as he swung onto his parents' potholed, tree-lined driveway. Through the rain he saw the living room still lit up. The only vehicle out front was Gunsten's pickup. Gun's rented Dodge, damn the thing, hit bottom in a washed-out section of grade, and Gun took his foot off the gas, applied the brake. He relaxed his hands on the steering wheel and took a long breath. He'd overreacted. Everything out here looked fine, and now he'd have to turn around and drive back into town. Then an explosion crashed and died in the dead air—one more blast, and forty yards ahead Gun saw Carol burst through the wire-screen window of the porch door and land on her back on the front steps. She was moving, though, up and scrambling, running low to the ground toward the barn.

Gun speared the gas pedal and jerked the wheel to the right, putting the car on a line to cut off Carol from the house. The Dodge slid sideways in the wet grass and struck the hard maple Gunsten had planted fifty years ago. The cheap metal of the car's door crumpled inward. Window glass peppered Gun's face and hands. He shut off the engine, bailed out the passenger side, saw Carol crawling back toward him in the grass, reached out and pulled her to him and beneath him. He lay there next to the right front wheel of the car, holding onto Carol. Her breath was ripping in and out of her, shoulders bucking. He squeezed her hard and said straight down into her ear, "You're fine, now talk!"

"He came through the back door—shot the lock, God—I was out on the porch, getting my shoes—coming back in I saw him kick it open—your parents—" Carol's lungs sucked and heaved. "Your parents were up—your dad pushing your mom—God, toward the stairway—up."

"There were two shots," said Gun.

"He shot again—at them—I don't know—I was running. Gun—he's gonna kill them."

He lifted Carol and pushed her into the front seat of the Dodge. "Stay low. The keys are there, start it up, back up first—you can't go forward—and get to a phone. Go now!"

He slammed the door on her, jumped the hood of the car, and sprinted across the lawn toward the front door of the house. He heard the Dodge start up, and he spun around, yelling, *"Go, go!"* Saw the car leap backward from the maple tree, Carol's head snapping forward. Then he was through the porch and standing in the kitchen. Straight ahead was the back door, flung wide open. To the right was the empty living room, and beyond it the stairway leading to the second-floor bedrooms. No sound now but the Dodge winding out and gaining distance. He thought of his mom and dad's bedroom closet, where Gunsten had always kept the rifles and shotguns. Were they still there? Would there be any shells? Was there a lock on that old bedroom door?

A shot went off upstairs like the end of the world, dishes rattling in Madilyn's hutch, and Gun was taking the steps three at a time, not slowing at the landing or even as he reached the hallway.

Calvin was at the end of the hallway, at the end bedroom door, which was still closed, thank God. He turned from the door now, the big .45 smoking in his hand. He lifted the .45 toward Gun and fired. But Gun had lurched sideways into the bathroom and heard the *thuck* of lead slug meeting good plaster wall. Absurdly, as he stood in the bathtub pressing himself against the inside wall of the bathroom, he thought of his mother and the precision she exercised when wallpapering.

He said, loudly, "Calvin," but he didn't need to. Calvin was moving right in with a stiff-armed double grip on the .45. Gun's hand closed on a sopping washcloth and whipped it into Calvin's face. He heard another shot, this one lighting up the whole landscape of his brain, and drove forward, blind on his feet, nothing but a howling black light in his eyes. He came down on the tile floor, Calvin wild beneath him. He went for the man's throat, found it, took hold, then lost it when something unforgivingly hard struck the crown of his head.

It was a momentary loss of control to pain, then Gun shook himself and sat up blinking, his eyes seeing again. He saw Calvin standing above him in front of the old claw-footed bathtub. There was confusion in that remarkably indistinct face of his. Nevertheless Calvin was sighting down the barrel of the .45 revolver, the bore was so large it seemed to offer a tunnel of escape. Calvin's hands were steady. Gun could think of not one sensible word.

Yet a voice did speak, a deep voice from the hallway.

"Put the gun away, son." It was Gunsten. In his hands was the Winchester Model 12 shotgun he'd always used for geese. Gunsten's eyes were deep and dark inside his head—he might have been speaking from another world. "Put it down, Calvin. Please."

But Calvin drew back the hammer of the .45, and Gunsten's shotgun boomed. Calvin spun away into the shattering, blistering-yellow sound.

Even before the noise had leaked out the walls and left the house in peace Gun was moving his arms and legs, his neck and fingers, checking to be sure every part was still there. Every part was. Enormously satisfied with this discovery, Gun looked around and found Calvin sprawled one-armed on the toilet. His other arm, its hand still grasping the .45, was lying on the pink tiles of the bathroom floor.

"Madilyn," said Gunsten, speaking calmly, "we need a wrap here, a belt or something. We don't want this boy losing too much blood. Our son's okay."

Gun's mother entered the bathroom faster than Gun's eyes could follow and went to work telling Calvin what to do, laying him down, getting his feet up on a pillow, yanking snug a belt on his shoulder to stop the flow of blood. Calvin was nodding, crying, his eyes shooting around inside his head. Madilyn smoothed his hair.

Gun heard sirens now as Gunsten knelt down beside him. Gun said, "I'm not sure I can stand up yet, Dad."

"Then sit for a while," his father told him.

# 36

*Every few nights toward morning, all summer long, it comes sliding into Gun's mind, sending him into a sweat, playing itself out mercilessly and finally waking him. But now the dream is peopled with faces Gun can name. The rain falling steadily on the ballfield grass. The silent boys struggling—Harry and Calvin Summers. Harry being struck down, falling. Then the flat sound of spade slamming into wet sod, and filthy dead-faced Neb, handling that spade with an efficiency born of despair.*

The picture was more complete than incomplete, yet knowing who killed whom and how the one had come to lie for so long in a hidden grave, this was not enough. June, July, and part of August had passed, and now Gun expected that his parents would have some of the answers to the questions he still had.

Two days ago they'd called. Madilyn called, actually, with surprising and sad news. After two months of silence, and just a week before the start of his trial, Calvin Summers had summoned a reporter from the Houghton paper. With a tape recorder running, Calvin had given a full confession. Then that night he'd hanged himself in his cell, using a rope he'd braided from a pair of blue jail pants. Gun didn't have the whole story yet, only the little his mother had said over the phone and a pair of short wire pieces from the paper. He would learn more today; late last night Gunsten and Madilyn had arrived from Michigan.

Here on Stony Lake, autumn came first to the massive old three-stemmed birch tree down along the shoreline beside the dock. Its leaves started fading in mid-July, and now with August arrived they were in full color and dropping themselves thickly onto the shaded water below, carpeting it yellow. The birch had been here from the first, already a good-sized adult when Gun bought the property twenty-five years ago. With each passing year it seemed to shed its green earlier. This bothered Gun some. Autumn bothered him, for that matter, though he loved the season and its colors, its flights of northern ducks and sharp, cool smells. So much beauty, he thought, and so transient —as he supposed beauty must be. He wondered if the season would feel any different to him this time around.

He reached into the breast pocket of his blue work shirt and brought out tobacco and papers. For long years Gun's habit had been to roll and smoke the day's first cigarette at the kitchen table, his reward for having done his morning push-ups. Now there were other things to consider. Like the fact that Carol preferred to sleep in but was not able to if her nose detected smoke in the air. Sitting out here on the dock, witnessing the first moments of a new day, Gun thought, *Small price.*

It was five-forty-five, the sun not yet showing itself above the tops of the high, virgin pines to the east, and Gun had been up for an hour. The dream had wakened him early, and rather than try to sleep again with his mind fastened on death, Gun had risen and walked down to the lake in darkness. He entered the water and swam across to a point of sandy soil where roses grew wild and cut a bouquet of some three dozen, along with greens and a few small white flowers he couldn't name. He swam the quarter mile home on his back, slowly, drinking the smell of the flowers that rode on his chest. He arranged them in a metal watering can he found in the garage and set them out on the front step.

The cool water and the work of swimming, the smell of the flowers, the image in his mind of Carol finding them—it all helped to break the dream's hold, to free up Gun's lungs, to clear his mind of the pictures and sounds he didn't want there.

Gun finished his cigarette and walked up the gentle grassy slope toward the log house. Rounding the southwest corner, he saw Gunsten step from the front door and bend to sniff the roses Gun had left on the steps.

"Morning. Like the flowers I picked?"

His father straightened slowly—this took some time, all that height. Both of his hands went to the small of his back. He laughed and raised long arms in a gesture of grand statement. "What marriage will do to a man," he said.

It wasn't much to look at from the outside, but to Gun it represented much of what he loved about this part of the world. The lack of pretension. The quiet.

The opposition to change for the mere sake of change. It was a low building set among birch trees, Stony Lake in the canvas behind, a green neon sign in the window saying, Jack-Be-Nimble's. When you walked inside your eyes had to wait for a while before they could tell you what you were seeing. The interior was dark, with golden knotty pine all around, high wooden booths along two walls, a long mahogany bar along another. Pool tables in back. Jack kept things neat and for the most part clean. He never changed the decor. There were fish mounted on polished slabs of oak: walleyes, northerns, one big muskie. And though Hamms Beer in the blue cans might be gone forever, Jack still had his lighted shadow box with its pear-shaped Hamms Bear character inside, paddling a canoe across sky-blue waters. Above the center of the bar was a bull moose with antlers seven feet from tip to tip. Once a tourist from Minneapolis had said to Jack how sad it was that someone had killed such a fine creature and stuffed it like a piece of furniture.

"Tragic all right." Jack had said to the man. "Sit down, grieve over a beer."

Normally, Jack didn't open for business until one in the afternoon. But when he'd learned that Gun's parents were coming he'd insisted that Gun bring them over for breakfast. "Don't get a chance to do many breakfasts," he said, "and it's my favorite meal."

Walking in, Gun smelled the grill, heard the sizzling. Something from a pig, something smoked. He saw, too, that Jack had pushed his little round tables with their red-and-white-checked tablecloths out of the way and brought in a long rectangular one overlaid with white linen. Jack himself was dressed in his usual white apron and white V-necked T-shirt. His short arms were hairy and knotted with muscle. His black hair was shorn close to his head. He needed a shave.

Smiling broadly, he said, "Madilyn, you're lovely, and Gunsten, you're still tall."

Then he motioned toward the white table with an open hand. "Carol, Gun—being that I never got around to a wedding present . . ."

They talked first of the wedding, though there wasn't much to be said about it. Small—only Carol, Gun, and the preacher who lived down the road. Quick—four and a half minutes. Simple—Gun's backyard, wild daisies for flowers, no music save for the red-winged blackbirds squawking in the reeds. And no honeymoon, either. The island trip they would take next winter.

Then the conversation turned to Calvin Summers. Madilyn did the talking and Gunsten the nodding, though once in a while he tossed forth a small embellishment.

In his last two months of life Calvin had recuperated from the loss of his arm and apparently recovered his need to speak the truth. In the taped interview, which Madilyn and Gunsten had been allowed to hear, Calvin admitted without qualification to killing Harry Summers and Rick Dandrie. Also to blackmailing his father. As for Dandrie, it turned out Rufus had figured things right—the rub had been money, a drug-buying loan. It had been a simple matter of Calvin getting Dandrie drunk and then drowning him.

Calvin's blackmailing of his father, however, wasn't quite as easy to understand, Madilyn said. She sat for a moment, breathing quietly. Gun thought she looked tired this morning, the skin surrounding her eyes darker and slacker than what a single late night or long drive could account for. And though for years she'd seemed immune to graying, Gun thought he saw more white strands among the brown.

"What did Calvin say about it in the interview?" Carol asked.

"Not much," said Madilyn. "Something like, 'How could Dad do that to me?' And really, when you think about it, it's quite a thing, what Neb did. A father putting a bushel over his son that way, expecting him to stay inside it and breathe that used-up air all his life. Calvin just couldn't live that way after a while."

"Poisoned," said Gunsten.

Everyone was silent. They'd finished eating and were on their second cups of coffee. Jack was sitting back in his chair, arms crossed, looking admiringly from empty plate to empty plate.

"Did Neb actually get the fifty thousand and deliver it?" Carol asked.

"He got some of it together, yes. About ten thousand, according to Calvin, some of it from the uncle in Toronto. And yes, he delivered it, too. Of course, whether or not Neb knew who it was, we'll never learn."

That's why Neb left the blackmail note for someone to find. Gun thought. Maybe he'd learned that his own boy was bleeding him out. Maybe allowing the truth at the end was both redemption and revenge.

Gun said, "What bothers me is not knowing what happened between Calvin and Harry. How Neb got involved. And Green Tokannah."

Madilyn shook her head. Her eyes were distant. "One thing leading to another . . ."

"The smallest difference in timing and nothing at all would've happened," said Gunsten. He shrugged and looked at his wife.

"Neb dropped Calvin off at a friend's house that night for a party," Madilyn started, "Then, after the school board meeting, Neb decided to stop by and pick him up on the way home. Except when he got there Calvin was gone. His friends said he'd run over

241

to the ballfield to find his wallet. There'd been a pickup game that afternoon, and Calvin thought he'd left it there in the dugout. Of course, when Neb reached the ballfield you know what he found."

"How did Calvin and Harry end up at the ballfield together?" Gun asked.

Gunsten lifted a finger. "Here's what I meant about timing."

Madilyn said, "You know where Harry lived. It's just a few blocks from the ballfield. He was on his way out to the lake that night, by foot, to our place. Bound for Canada. He was walking along the edge of town so nobody would see him, and he went right behind the bleachers there, past the dugout where Calvin was searching for his wallet. Calvin said he just knew right away what Harry was up to. He didn't even have to ask. They started arguing. He said he couldn't remember how the fighting began or how many times they hit each other. He just remembered the rage he felt. Not because Harry was going to Canada, or anything like that. But because Harry was leaving, doing something Calvin knew *he* couldn't do. All the years growing up, trying to keep up with his cousin and not being able to, and now Harry was just up and leaving him for good."

"So he killed him?" said Gun.

Madilyn tilted her face to one side and nodded, tentative. "He didn't intend to. He said he threw Harry's pack to the ground, and the stuff inside scattered. Your father's hammer was there—Harry was returning it. Then they were wrestling each other in the grass, and everything was crazy. Calvin said he must have grabbed the hammer. . . ." Madilyn lifted her narrow-fingered hands from the table and looked at them. They were lovely, Gun thought.

"When Neb showed up he drove Calvin home. Dropped him a couple blocks from the house with orders to tell his mother he'd walked. Then Neb went back to do what he'd decided had to be done. Green was at school late and thought he saw something on the ballfield, walked down there and found Neb digging the hole in back of the dugout. Saw the body. There was no way for him to figure Calvin into it. And Neb must've kept that part to himself."

Jack picked this moment to snap his shoulders back and knock his knuckles on the table. "Time for more coffee. And don't be thinking I forgot dessert, either." He stood and walked quickly to the bar. He grabbed the large stainless-steel electric pot and flourished it.

Carol said, "It's hard to know who to feel the most sorry for."

Gingerly, with all ten fingers, Madilyn lifted her coffee cup and held it out for Jack to fill. "The whole lot of them," she said.

# 37

*E*arly morning.

In the distance, beyond the expanse of longish grass dotted with pines, a heavy mist rises from the lake. The air here is infused with the yellowish, almost smoky light of a brand-new August northern sun. The dew is heavy and has soaked through Gun's tennis shoes. He is wearing, besides the shoes, only a pair of gray long johns.

Already he has loaded his pitching machine with a dozen new baseballs, and he stands content now at the white rock he uses for home plate. On his right shoulder rests a long blond bat, Hillerich and Bradsby. His hands are relaxed on the narrow handle. His knees are bent slightly. He has shifted his weight to his rear leg. The machine, which he built for himself years ago, ticks away, its steel arm moving upward incrementally. As the arm nears horizontal Gun lifts the bat and tucks in his front shoulder. The steel arm leaps, and the ball comes fast and true, a little more than waist-high. Gun strides and swings, nothing in his mind or eye but the ball and its rotating red seams—nothing in the world but that, and the power of such absolute reduction slows time, almost stopping the ball in flight and allowing Gun the required grace. He hears the wooden pop and watches the white sphere sail off into a blue sky populated with green pines.

A few seconds later Gun hears the small sound of ball striking water. He senses a presence behind him. He turns, still unaccustomed to seeing a face in his own kitchen window.

Author of the Edgar Award-nominee *Comeback*

# L.L. ENGER

"Enger writes a...sharp, engaging story.
Pedersen is a complicated main character...
it's quite a ride to tag along with him."
—*Minneapolis Star Tribune*

## THE GUN PEDERSEN MYSTERIES

# SWING

# COMEBACK

# STRIKE

# SACRIFICE

# Jeremiah Healy

## A John Cuddy Mystery

# Foursome

POCKET
BOOKS

**Available in hardcover from Pocket Books**